CODE NAME: DAEDALUS

SHANE O'BRIEN MACDONALD

Ankerville Street Productions
North America

First digital edition May 2014
ISBN: 978-0-9920080-3-1
First trade paperback edition May 2014
ISBN: 978-0-9920080-2-4

Found an error in one of our books? Don't get angry, have us fix it! Contact:
Ankerville Street Productions North America
ankervillestreetprods@gmail.com

Cover design by Yukiko Sato

FROM INSIDE THE NOVEL...

This is where things got a bit weird. Meisner was still wearing a towel-Kiki saw Tatyana's hand disappear under it. An instant later the man's face shot up in agony:

"AAAAhhhhhhhhhaaaaaa...what are you doing?"

Tatyana had latched on to one of his more delicate parts. "You don't like my technique?" she asked.

"Uh-uh."

"We want to know," said Tatyana, "who you've been ferrying."

Meisner squirmed. "What do you mean? I don't know what you're talking about."

Kiki saw Tatyana's wrist make another twist. Kiki leaned down. She was face-to-face with the guy. "Look, I don't like what she's doing either, but this is going to go on until she gets what she wants. We know who you are, what you do, and we've been reading your e-mails for the last six weeks. We've got a pretty good picture of your activities, and your friends. We don't care what you're doing. We don't want to have any contact with you, at all. But we're looking for someone, who you escorted to the airport this morning. We know you don't know his name. We just want to know where he was going."

Meisner was silent.

Kiki leaned in and whispered. "She's ripped them off before. Never on purpose. But accidents happen, you know. But that was in Minsk."

ONLY ONE WOMAN CAN STOP A DOOMSDAY MACHINE, MENACING THE EARTH FROM 50,000 FEET... ...AND THAT'S KIKI CLAYMORE!

Daedalus. A top-secret drone program. Completely self-sufficient, it has been hijacked by a group of terrorists. They want to turn it into a flying nuclear bomb—aiming it right at New York City. Their leader? The most recent ex-boyfriend of a young woman named Kiki Claymore.

She's the latest recruit of Task Force Ten—an ultra secret group of NATO secret agents. Her mission: find her former lover and stop him at all costs. The only problem? None of her fellow spies trust her. Is she on a mission to stop the man who broke her heart? Or will she betray her NATO colleagues to keep her love alive?

From faking her way through the red light district of Barcelona to a deadly shootout at mission control in Cape Canaveral—Kiki Claymore is on assignment to stop the only man she's ever loved. Before he unleashes a holocaust that will kill millions.

CHAPTER 1.1

There was not a star in the sky over the eastern coast of Maine. A dark and unforgiving area over the North Atlantic Ocean. The drone flew slowly, well below the sound barrier. Surveying the last bit of the American border before it would circle around and head back to the air base at Fort Kent. Undetectable to ordinary radar. Engines specially designed to muffle sound. Technology so new and experimental that the engineers struggled to find its limits. It was also a thing of beauty. With none of the ordinary constraints of an aircraft that carried passengers or cargo. Its designers were free to mold its bodywork in a manner that maximized fuel use. But the truth was that, unfortunately, it resembled a flying dolphin. Or a tadpole. Not so much a bird.

It was designed to fly sub-orbitally, as well as at altitudes barely eclipsing the treetops. This feature, more than anything, was what the manufacturing engineers said had eaten up the project's budget. After all, it was designed to be fully self-sufficient for three days in the event of a nuclear war.

What it was not well designed for was detecting other aircraft. That is how the Hercules DC-130H, some six thousand feet above, was able to creep up on the drone. The back of the plane opened up and spat out a lone figure, garbed all in black. The man, falling to earth, whose name was Ridley, felt the rush of air around his body as he fell towards the drone. His helmet was equipped with night vision technology that made the drone's fuselage turn white against the blackness of the ocean below.

Aerodynamic webbing stretched between his arms and torso. An outfit lifted from a comic book. But this was no laughing matter. If he made even the slightest mistake he would crash into the sea. If he were lucky enough to survive the fall, there would be no chance of rescue. He would drift with the Labrador Current until he hit land. Or was spotted by a passing cargo ship.

8000 feet...

7000...

6000...

It took a great deal of effort to push his arms together. His left hand reached over and turned a dial, attached to the wrist of his right glove. The glass plating of his helmet came alive with digital information, overlaying the green glow of the night vision. Now he knew his exact trajectory, altitude and speed.

Sweat trickled down his cheek. Alone, in the middle of the night, over an empty ocean. He was the first person to ever use this technology. His was the only suit. Ever to be used in the field. If something went wrong, it was probably going to go wrong for him.

On his back he felt the warmth and vibrations of his jetpack starting up. There had been long talks with the man who engineered the suit. If he survived this stage, the chance of death dropped dramatically. There was a very narrow window of thirty seconds for the computer to guide him into position over the drone. If any of the sensors were calibrated wrong... if any line of computer code had a mistake... if any bit of wiring caught fire... he would be going for a late night swim. The water below was barely above freezing.

If he didn't approach the drone at the right spot, at exactly the right angle and speed, he could find himself obliterated in the wake of a jet turbine.

The roar of the two engines in close proximity deafened his ears. Slowly the overlay on his helmet display changed. Lining up with the drone below him. The machine had no idea a human being was about to land on top of it. Its designers had never considered the possibility. The drone's sensors would indicate something was happening, but it had no way of processing this data. So it would simply ignore it. For all the sophistication of its computers, it could only understand what its creators had intended it to.

Ridley got closer and closer and closer. His suit had guided him within an arm span of the drone. Now it was his turn. Magnetic grips in his hands, arms and legs latched on to the metal body below him.

The computer in his suit immediately disabled the jet engine on his back. Lines of code scrolled down his helmet's display. The software in his suit was invading the drone's control system. An alarm went off in his ear.

4

The drone's engine cut out.

In mid-air the craft began to fall towards the earth. With all its power disabled, it swung around and began to topple end over end, down to the ocean.

CHAPTER 1.2

Lieutenant Auster's skin gushed in the sweltering Florida heat. It was a long way from his home base in eastern Germany. There the average summer temperature was around twenty-five degrees Celsius. He had gone outside for a cigarette. Because smoking was treated like a cardinal sin in America. Those terrible smokers had to go out into the thirty-five degree weather. Only to come back to a room where the air conditioning was set to a temperature slightly above what was acceptable for a refrigerator. So Americans could die from lung cancer caused by air pollution as opposed to lung cancer caused by cigarette smoke. Made all the worse by his struggle to translate from the American system of Fahrenheit. It always sounded like the nights would be cooler than they actually were. He was certain of one thing, though.

Ninety-five was extremely hot. And that was before the weatherman factored in the humidity.

One month of this exchange down, three more to go. That was the official schedule.

He had barely passed through the doors to the cavernous control room when one of the blue-shirted technicians rushed over to him. "We're having some problems with surveillance drone AU-187."

"Where is that located?"

"It's a border drone. Off the east coast."

"What do you mean by a problem?"

"The visual signal cut out."

"Was it observing something important?"

"No, it was over the ocean."

They rushed over to one of the pods of workstations that were set up in the middle of the room. "Show me the sequence of events that happened."

The technician flicked through a series of screens, each being fed data from the drone. "First," said the technician, "an air pressure alarm went off. It looks like some sort of downdraft hit the top of the fuselage. Then the video camera went. Now we're getting intermittent signals from the GPS."

"Could it be a mechanical problem?" Auster leaned towards the monitor. "AU-187. This is the Daedalus model, is it not?"

"Yes."

"This one is not equipped with a nuclear weapon, is it?"

The tech shook his head. "We're checking right now. But I'm almost certain it isn't."

"Almost certain?"

An awkward pause. "Should I wake up Vice-Admiral McGraw?"

"No. Let us handle it here. Until we're absolutely certain. This could be the weather. Or a temporary mechanical malfunction. See if we can get an uplink to the tracking station." Auster peered up to the map displayed on one of the enormous wall screens. "What are we looking at here? There's a beacon in Calais, Maine. And another in Fort Kent. Contact the control station there."

"Will do, sir."

"And make sure you do it quickly. Is the autodestruct ready as well?"

"Autodestruct is still on line, sir."

"Good. Be prepared to receive the order."

CHAPTER 1.3

The drone plummeted like a missile. At the front, Ridley's weight had stopped it from tumbling end over end. Now, it was headed straight downwards. Inside the helmet, computer code flashed, over and over, in bright red letters. In the corner of the display, an altimeter. It kept going down. 3200...3100...3000...

A giant roar cut through the wind noise. In the helmet entire sequences of symbols, numbers and unintelligible words flashed by. The drone's jet engine fired up and the craft began to level off. In the helmet the display changed from red to green. The lines of code went away. Airplane controls appeared. Like some ancient video game. Ridley manipulated the controls by applying the correct amount of pressure through his gloves. He could guide the rocket up and down. Pitch and yaw, left and right, all the controls were working perfectly.

He hoped the GPS was functioning properly. Of course, to Ridley, properly meant it was hiding his location. He scrolled down on the menu. Got a bearing. A map of eastern North America appeared. He zoomed in and found his exact location.

He was ready to set the autopilot. He aimed towards the northwest and flew off over the Canadian border.

CHAPTER 1.4

"What the hell's going on in here?"

Vice-Admiral McGraw's voice boomed across the room. Twenty-five faces ripped away from their monitors and turned towards the doorway. McGraw stood there, his uniform half-open. His white navy T-shirt exposed. He was angry.

Auster popped his head up. "Well, you see—"

"I don't want to see anything. You tell me what the hell's going on."

"We've lost contact with one of the drones."

"What do you mean we've lost contact? You don't just lose contact."

"Well, it was...the one..."

"Speak up, goddammit."

"I'm sorry, English is not my first language—"

"I don't care. You were supposed to

goddamn well know it when you got this assignment. What is your name?"

"Auster, sir. Lieutenant Auster. I'm from the German army and I'm—"

"No one gives a rat's ass, Auster. You tell me what's going on or you'll be manning a desk in the hall for the next four months."

Auster cleared his throat. "We lost contact with the drone off the coast of Maine. It seems to have disappeared off the radar. I mean, the location beacon's signal disappeared. Before it vanished we received telemetry that indicated it was plunging toward the ocean."

"What do you mean—plunging?"

"It started to freefall, end over end."

McGraw turned to the nearest tech. "What have we got on this aircraft?"

The technician opened a clipboard and flipped through some pages. "It's unmanned vehicle AU-187."

"Aquarius or Phoenix class?"

"No sir, it's Daedalus."

McGraw's eyes widened. "Daedalus? Oh my god..."

Auster moved in. "I don't understand—"

"You're damn right you don't." McGraw looked around nervously. "There's only one of those. If that one disappears, we're going to have three ships out there for the next two weeks. Trying to recover it." McGraw turned back to the technician. "Is there going to be anything left to find if it crashes?"

The tech shook his head. "I don't know sir. There is supposed to be a beacon with a two-month power supply, but we're not getting the signal. There could be interference."

"Like hell. Something here stinks and I don't want to take another whiff."

Auster grabbed the tech's clipboard. "We have telemetry until three thousand feet—"

"Oh my god." McGraw whipped around. "This is a disaster. Why didn't you wake me up?"

Auster assumed an apologetic tone. "Well, I didn't want to be waking up the Vice-Admiral without making sure—"

"Don't make sure, goddamnit. I'm just down the goddamn hall." He turned to the tech. "You get Admiral Hanson on the horn. We may have a problem."

"What do you mean?" asked Auster.

"I've got to find out if that sucker was flying nuclear. There could be enough firepower in that thing to take out half the cities in this country."

CHAPTER 2.1

"I don't want to dress like a slut," said Kiki.

Tatyana handed her a garter belt. "Well, you have no choice. It's part of the job. Besides, this is one of the finest exotic massage parlors in Barcelona."

"I didn't sign up for this." They were in the back of a concrete building at the south end of Las Rablas. The locals referred to it as Chinatown. But Kiki hadn't seen any Asians. Just a lot of scantily clad Easter European women. And sex shops.

"Look, it's very important. This guy, we've

spent two weeks trying to track him down. He's the only person who's had verifiable communications with your ex-boyfriend. And if we don't get him, there's going to be a lot of pressure on me to make up for your misgivings. You understand?"

Kiki examined the garter. "I don't understand how I'm supposed to put this on." She looked down at her legs. She was wearing Lycra panties with a dark purple corset. What little chest she had was being thrust up towards her throat. She could barely breath. European lingerie designers were clearly not worried about practicality. "What am I supposed to do with these?" There was no obvious way to connect the garter to the black stockings.

"Haven't you ever dressed up for sex before?"

"That's not how it works back home. We take our clothing off, not the other way around." Kiki shook the stockings in anger. "Look, I'm not a stripper."

"Well, maybe you should be. You could use a little grounding in the real world." Tatyana was wearing something that resembled a bikini mated with a tentacle monster. "Here. Give it to me."

Tatyana leaned down and guided the garter on,

shoving her gigantic bust in Kiki's face. She grimaced and strained her neck back as Tatyana attached the stockings.

When Tatyana finally moved away Kiki relaxed. "How many times have you done this?"

"This is one of our most useful methods. Mostly since our male counterparts are useless. From this very massage parlor we've gotten no less than three leads. Including one that outed a double agent working within the task force. Although I'm not supposed to talk about that."

Kiki sighed.

"Don't worry," said Tatyana. "Just remember—if he touches you, don't push his hands away. You got that? If you don't like what he's doing, just casually step backward. Don't touch him with your hands, except his back. Leave the touching to me. Okay?"

"You mean I'm going to have to touch his back?"

"It's not going to be all that bad. For all we know, this guy will be ravenously handsome. It might be a real labor of love."

Kiki rolled her eyes. "Right."

An elderly Korean woman entered. "Look. He's here."

Tatyana rustled through her bag. "Let me get the binoculars."

They both headed to the only window in the room—a narrow horizontal slit in the concrete. It looked directly out onto the parking lot. Gave the room a bunker-like ambiance.

"Hmmm," said Tatyana. "Here he comes. Over by the blue BMW. He visits here like clockwork, twice a week. The man sitting in the car is his driver and bodyguard. He always waits in the parking lot while the target gets um, his business done."

"What's our guy's name?"

"Meisner." Tatyana put down her binoculars.

"So he's a German."

"I think so."

"You think this scam will actually work?"

"Trust me. It has never failed. Not since god created woman." Tatyana smiled. "Once you've learned some of the moves I have, you'll always get what you want."

CHAPTER 2.2

"Girls—come say hello," the Korean woman shouted in heavily accented Spanish.

Kiki and Tatyana wandered out of the staff room. They entered the main lobby, which was palatially decorated in ancient Egyptian style.

"Girls," said the Korean woman, "why don't you introduce yourselves?"

Kiki stepped forward first. "Hi, I'm Jasmine."

"I'm Candy," said Tatyana.

"Hmm, I don't know," said Meisner. "I think I'm hungry for Candy."

"Oh, but you want to have us both, don't you?" said Kiki as she took his arm.

Tatyana ran a finger down his chest. "Yeah. It'll be more fun with the both of us. We do a really good job together."

Meisner bit his lip. "But it's kind of expensive."

Kiki leaned in towards his ear. "We'll give you a discount." She moved around and gazed directly into his eyes, doe-like. Meisner held her glance for a moment. He was realizing how cute she actually was.

"Well," he said, "I suppose we can do that."

Tatyana smiled. "Now you go in and shower and we'll be there in two shakes of a lamb's tail."

Meisner smiled. "See you shortly." The Korean lady escorted him away.

"Do you think he bought it?"

Tatyana rolled her eyes. "Of course he did." She headed back to the break room. Kiki followed. "You're learning. Using your face was a good idea. It's your strongest asset. Work with it."

Tatyana made a quick call to headquarters in Amsterdam. Tin Man was on the other line. "Okay," he said, "We're all ready on this end."

"What are you seeing?"

"Things I rather not. I'd prefer not to be gazing at a man undressing on a hidden camera," he said, his British accent putting a particular emphasis on the 'P' sound. In the Amsterdam office Tin Man was watching a false-color heat image. It was one of their tools to find out if an interrogation subject was giving information they believed to be true. "Mr. Meisner is more chickadee than elephant, if you know what I'm saying."

Tatyana shook her head. "As long as he has the correct equipment, that's all that counts."

Tin Man smiled. "So, you girls are going to get naked, right?"

Kiki shook her head at the thought. "No way. That's not going to happen."

"All part of the surprise," said Tatyana. "I don't want you running off in the middle of things, going for coffee."

"Absolutely not," said Tin Man, "I only drink tea when I'm on the continent."

"You're sure everything's fine? Nothing needs adjustment?"

"The camera and transmitter are working beautifully."

A few minutes later Kiki and Tatyana entered the massage room. It was dark and the air was heavy in the immediate aftermath of a shower. Meisner lay face down on the massage table, eyes closed. He'd left his towel draped over his behind. As Kiki got closer her nose detected a distinct—and unpleasant—smell. How much garlic had this guy eaten for lunch? she wondered. It wasn't just that—she walked in and wondered why he was still wearing a T-shirt. Up closer, she discovered she was looking at Meisner's back hair. A thick forest. The man looked like he had been birthed by a gorilla.

The guy totally grossed her out. As one of the regular girls told her when she was preparing, "That's why we take lots of showers. You get used to it, cleansing yourself from the ick."

"Wow, isn't he lovely," said Tatyana.

"Such a toned body," Kiki lied, massaging the back of his neck. She pushed towards his back. His skin was rough. Like sandpaper. What had this guy done to himself? Spent every day in the sun? If she had to do this for a half hour, she'd have no skin left on the palms of her hands.

Tatyana was working Meisner's legs. Then Kiki felt him awkwardly trying to touch her stomach. "Where are you from?" he asked Kiki.

"I'm an exchange student from California."

"Hmmm," he said. "I love Hollywood. Have you ever been in a movie?"

"Yeah, I have," said Kiki. "It was a naughty movie." Tatyana shot her a look. As if to say she was going a bit overboard with the ruse. Stop it before you give us both away.

"Me and my boyfriend made it," said Kiki, attempting a recovery. "Fortunately he didn't put it on the internet."

"Ah, that's too bad," said Meisner.

It was at that point that Kiki felt his hand running up from her knee towards her crotch. Before he could get his hands on anything delicate she backed off and moved to the other side of the table, taking up his right arm.

"Well, are you interested in something extra?" asked Tatyana.

"Yeah," he said. "But it sounds a bit expensive."

"I'll bet you'll pay anything for pleasure."

Meisner laughed. "Maybe you're right."

This is where things got a bit weird. Meisner was still wearing a towel-Kiki saw Tatyana's hand disappear under it. An instant later the man's face shot up in agony:

"AAAAhhhhhhhhhaaaaaa...what are you doing?"

Tatyana had latched on to one of his more delicate parts. "You don't like my technique?" she asked.

"Uh-uh."

Leaning down, Kiki locked eyes with the guy. "Look, I don't like what she's doing either, but we know who you are, what you do, and we've been reading your e-mails for the last six weeks. We've got a pretty good picture of your activities, and your friends. We don't care what you're doing. We don't want to have any contact with you, at all. But we're looking for someone, who you escorted to the airport this morning. We know you don't know his name. We just want to know where he was going."

Meisner was silent.

Kiki leaned in and whispered. "She's ripped them off before. Never on purpose. But accidents happen, you know... But that was in Minsk."

"In Belarus?" Meisner was panicked.

"That's a secret. Don't tell anyone."

"The man... he was going to Lima... Lima... in Peru. He's already gone. He was on the eleven-thirty flight."

"The name," said Kiki. "The name, please."

"I don't know. He didn't even speak. He just took his ticket and left.

"What does he do?"

"He's a banker. From an English-speaking country. That's all I know, I swear."

She patted him on the head. "You've been a good boy. Promise you won't tell your bodyguard about us. If he starts any trouble, our boss will get angry. Which means we'll get angry with you, okay?"

Meisner nodded.

"We might not be able to find you, that's true." Kiki narrowed her gaze. "But we might. Okay? We don't care what you do, as long as it doesn't involve me or her. Right, Candy?"

Tatyana smiled. "Right."

Kiki went back to the break room and contacted Tin Man on the satellite hookup, "So?"

"Well, it looks like he's telling the truth. The heat topography seems to bear it out."

She returned to Tatyana. "He's clean. Leave him the envelope."

"What?" asked Meisner.

"Don't turn around," said Tatyana. "We're leaving you a special surprise. A thousand Euros for all your hard work."

He was speechless.

"We won't tell anybody if you don't," said Kiki.

"Another girl will be in shortly," said Tatyana. "She doesn't know about any of this, so don't ask. And if you say anything but 'good-bye' to the owner, we'll make your life miserable. Okay?"

"We just got hired," said Kiki. "You're our first customer. And our last. So don't take it out on the establishment."

"They want your business. They love your business."

Back in the break room, Kiki struggled to get the garter belt off. "Now what?"

"We'll know in two hours once the Committee makes their decision."

"What are the chances that one of us is going to Peru?"

CHAPTER 2.3

Two hours later Kiki and Tatyana were back at the hotel. Task Force Ten had been kind enough to put them up at the Mandarin

Oriental, right in the center of Barcelona. Kiki marveled at the view out her window. She'd never been to Spain before. So many people in a city with such beautiful weather. For someone from a northern country, the fact that such a place existed was almost a miracle in itself.

They had arrived that morning. With barely enough time to check in before they headed out searching for Meisner. Now it seemed they had a bit more time on their hands.

"Listen, girls," said Digby, "Don't worry about it. You've done a very good job. We don't need you back here right now. Take a couple more days and stick around, okay? Just keep your eyes and ears open."

"You really think you need us here?" asked Tatyana.

Kiki had a less rhetorical question. "Do you want us to keep an eye on Meisner?"

"Let me worry about him. We need to check out this Peru business. There's been a lot of traffic coming from signals intelligence. If you can rely on that bunch. Half the time I think our liaison is stoned."

"Really?" said Tatyana. "That's the faith you put in people who bug phones?"

"Pretty much," said Digby. "Two more days. Stick around. Go see the city. And don't forget to bring me back some tortas Ines Rosales. You got that, Kiki? Two packs for everybody in the office."

"So I'm your courier, now?" she said.

"Basically, yes."

They ended the conversation and Kiki prepared to go back to her room. As she was leaving she turned to Tatyana. "This is a bit weird, but..."

"What?"

"When do we get paid, exactly?"

"You haven't gotten your paycheck, yet? I'm sure it'll be soon, if it hasn't happened today. It will be quite substantial."

"Is this what they do every time? They put us up in nice, four star hotels?"

"Pretty much. It's one of the perks for putting your life on the line. The last thing they want is to send us into a dangerous situation only to have us run out of money ten years later. And go write a book about it."

"Who would do something like that?"

"There are people. From the intelligence services. Gone on to write novels. Look at John LeCarre. Or that woman who used to head up the British Secret Service. I mean, there's a certain understanding that they'll take care of you if you behave and don't cause a fuss. If you don't start tattling, right?"

"Yeah, well, I still have to deal with a lot of family affairs back in Scotland."

"Well, the sooner we find your ex-boyfriend, the better." Tatyana reached for her purse. "Look, if money is an issue, I'll lend you some. If you need to go shopping or anything."

Kiki was about to get offended by the shopping comment, but decided that Tatyana, as superficial as she was, meant well. "Thanks, but I'll be fine."

"Okay. But I have to go."

"Where?" asked Kiki.

"I have a, um, friend, who wants to see me this evening."

"A... friend?"

"Don't tell me I have to report every rendezvous with you, do I?"

A little while later Kiki decided to wander around the neighborhood. Found a grocery store that sold a fairly decent selection of ice cream. She went back to her room and flicked through tourist brochures, picked up in the lobby. Barcelona. Pretty nice city. The parts designed by Antonio Gaudi looked incredible. It amazed Kiki how the city had let him get away with such crazy designs.

She was halfway through the stack of pamphlets when the room phone rang. Who the hell would be calling her here? She picked it up, expecting to hear the front desk clerk. "Hello?"

"Now you listen to me." She recognized the voice immediately. Meisner. The accent was unmistakable. "If I ever hear from you or your friend again, I'll kill you both. Don't think I don't have the people to do it. You understand?"

CHAPTER 2.4

Trees. Endless trees. Punctuated occasionally by swamp. And it wasn't like it was a variety of trees either—all spruce or fir or some other kinds of coniferous types. That was all Ridley had been able to see since the sun came up. He had been flying the drone as low as possible. Just on the off chance that he came into visual contact with another airplane. Someone nosy reporting things back. He was certain that the Canadian authorities did not have their own unmanned aircraft. So the Daedalus would arouse suspicion, especially with a jetpack-equipped man on top.

A couple of hours after sunrise Ridley detected the signal from the Val d'Or airport landing beacon. He was close. Now came the hard part. He had never been up here before, and he had to find the landing site. The organization had decided that the best place to hide the drone was an abandoned strip mine in Northern Quebec. The ground flat enough to make a decent approach. And the site had an abandoned warehouse that would function as a hangar. Few had questioned the mine's sale to a South American company several months previous. Fewer still when they delayed start of any future operations. That was the site's key advantage. Very few places would be as isolated, or so they believed. If they needed to get any special equipment or electronics, it was only a seven-hour journey to Montreal. At first they had considered the high arctic, but the risks outweighed the reduced chance of interference.

It had another key feature—the mine was, in aeronautical terms, extremely close to Montreal, Boston, and New York City. Each was a nice big fat ransom target. Ridley knew that one of those cities had been programmed into the software used to hijack the drone's controls. Probably New York. Once a ransom demand was sent, all the scrambled fighter jets and anti-aircraft guns would be useless. The Daedalus drone could be on top of anyone of those cities before government could retaliate.

As the early morning sunlight glared into his helmet, the GPS alarm went off. There, off in the distance, like a scar upon the landscape, was the copper mine. Abandoned more than twenty years ago. He was surprised that no one had bought it, given that the price of commodities had gone through the roof. Nonetheless, who was he to argue? He slowly guided the drone down. Hopefully the landing wouldn't be too rough.

However, unbeknownst to Ridley, down below Sergeant Michel Goudain of the Sureté du Quebec was driving home after a long night shift. Heading north on Route 113 along Lac Parent. He could barely contain his surprise at seeing the aircraft descend over the forest in front of him. At first he thought it was some sort of model plane. But who would have a model plane out at eight o'clock on a Tuesday morning? He saw it go down beyond the trees and knew exactly where it was going to land.

Oh, what the hell... He was curious to find out who would spend that kind of money on something. To fly around these parts. He'd go and check it out. Maybe the guy could give him a good price on one for his kids.

Meanwhile, Ridley was trying desperately to hang on for dear life in the shear from the crosswinds. KA-CLUNK! KA-CLUNK! KA-CLUNK! The drone was not designed to mitigate turbulence. Hardly a surprise for a craft designed without a crew. He descended below the trees and into the mine pit. At the last moment he realized that he was landing in the wrong spot—separated from the hangar by a giant slope as well as a great distance. He pulled up against the hill and shot over the pit. Saw his final approach. The wheels touched down.

The ground was mushy from a rainstorm the previous night. The aircraft shook violently. Despite the magnetic suit, he thought he was going to be thrown from the plane. An alarm was beeping. The plane wasn't slowing down properly. Finally he could see the mine's warehouse. He made a hard right, then forced the craft a little off to the left. The turning slowed the plane down. He cruised in, parking the craft about fifty meters from the warehouse door.

Well, that was terrifying, thought Ridley. But at least it's down. He carefully lowered the magnetic charge on his suit. He crawled over the top of the fuselage, onto the wing, and slid.

Finally, solid ground. He took off his helmet and walked to the warehouse. By a small side door he found a key and a cell phone. He hit the first number on the redial menu.

"Hello," he said. "Is this—?"

"Yes, of course," said the voice. "The code to open the warehouse is 5151825."

Ridley keyed it in to a small pad beside the door. It unlocked with a clang.

"All right, now hurry up," said the voice. "Don't take all day. Get that thing out of sight. The last thing we need is another nosy local."

Once inside Ridley opened the wide front doors. The place was more an aluminum barn than an actual aircraft hangar. It took a fair bit of heaving to get the large barn doors open. There was a small forklift in the back. He attached it to the front of the drone and dragged the craft inside. He had just gotten it parked and the doors closed when he heard the sound of a car pulling up.

Great, he thought, I don't even have a knife to defend myself. He peeked out through a dirt-smeared window. It was a cop. What the hell? This is not good.

The officer wandered around the site. What was he looking for? But the policeman didn't come anywhere near the landing strip or the barn. A good thing, too. He would have easily seen a line of tracks made by the drone's landing gear. Instead, he wandered around a bit more. To the edge of the woods, then back to his car.

When he was gone Ridley felt relief. Nonetheless, he telephoned back the Swede. "You don't understand what just happened to me. I've only been here five minutes and already a cop has pulled up."

"Don't worry. He probably saw the thing land, and was wondering what was going on. Did he come in? Did he knock?"

"No."

"Well, he probably doesn't care. I wouldn't worry. There's only three policemen in the town nearby. As far as they know, we're not doing anything illegal. Yet."

"I don't know. What if they come in here?"

"They can't search without probable cause. Bottom line is, don't panic. Now, I suggest that you deal with things immediately at hand. Supplies. You can go into the nearest town. Food, water, everything else you'll need, you can get there. We will arrive in two days."

"What about the specialist? Where's the device?"

"You should find it across from the side door." Ridley turned around and saw a large case made of carbon fiber. "I know what you're thinking. Don't open it," said the Swede.

"How are we getting the specialist out of Barcelona? Won't the authorities notice?

"Don't worry, leave that to us. You're part is done for now. We'll need you again shortly."

Ridley didn't like the Swede's condescending tone. "When am I going to get paid?"

"No need to worry. All in good time. Just relax until the specialist arrives. And don't go poking around, either. We wouldn't want something to explode by accident, would we?"

CHAPTER 3.1

Kiki hit the beach in the morning. She lay in the sun for about twenty minutes. Then a young man plopped down next to her. Started making conversation. Despite the fact that she was non-responsive, the guy kept on talking. When English got no response he switched to Spanish. Two minutes passed. He had pretty much given up when he took a quick swoop down and grabbed her bag. Immediately she grabbed his arm and kicked him straight in the ass. He screamed to high heaven and clutched his tailbone. The guy probably never imagined such a small girl could possibly pack such a wallop.

A while later she checked the time on her

phone. It was getting closer to eleven-thirty. She left the beach and took the subway to Eixample. She could get a nice view of the Segratta Familia there. She felt peckish as she wandered back to the hotel to change. A few blocks from the Mandarin she stumbled upon an American diner-style restaurant.

Hmm...burgers. They looked like they might be a step up from standard fast food fare. She'd been warned by Tatyana to be wary of the restaurants near the tourist areas. They tended to be outrageously overpriced, ranging from bland to terrible. And they didn't usually serve local food, anyway.

She decided to stop and take a quick look at the menu. Who did she spot on the other side of the room but Meisner. Tatyana had told her not to follow him. But this was an opportunity not to get caught.

While most of the tables in the center of the restaurant were open concept, the walls were ringed by booths. High booths. Just tall enough that she could conceal her identity from Meisner if she approached from the right direction.

She surreptitiously snuck over and sat down behind where Meisner was seated with his bodyguard and a third man. They hadn't noticed her, and continued their conversation without interruption. They were talking about ski resorts in southern Switzerland.

She flipped through the menu. The waitress arrived and she ordered a coffee in Spanish. After a couple of minutes the conversation fell silent and she heard the sound of an envelope being opened.

"These are all the details of the man you need to find, okay? You understand?" said Meisner.

"You're sure everything's here? And you've already put the money in my account?" asked the man.

"Mr. Lansing, we would always make sure you are properly compensated for your hard work. If this contract goes smoothly, we look forward to working with you again."

So he had a name, thought Kiki.

"The man you'll be escorting will not be very hard to find. Hopefully this job will take you no more than a few hours."

"You know that the authorities will be on my tail. From the moment I clear customs," said Lansing.

Meisner chuckled. "That is precisely what we are counting on. You are our red herring. Our juicy cut of meat to be thrown to the Doberman while we climb over the fence. By the time they're finished retracing your steps, we'll be long gone."

"Sounds easy enough to me."

"Just be careful. We've already had incidents with foreign agents who tried to interfere. These people get physical, in the sneakiest ways. So no diversions until the job is done, okay?"

"Sure."

The waitress arrived with Kiki's coffee order. She heard Lansing get up, say good-bye. She decided to cancel it. Now, had any other agent been there, they would have told her to phone in a report. The last thing she should do is start a pursuit. But Kiki didn't know the rules.

Meisner immediately got suspicions when he heard her voice. Canceling the coffee order in English. Kiki didn't know how to do it in Spanish.

Meisner was still super self-conscious after the previous day's incident. He got up and took a look around. Anger filled him as he saw who was paying at the cash register.

He gestured towards his bodyguard. "Stop her."

CHAPTER 3.2

Kiki walked out of the restaurant. She made her way down the Grand Via and decided to turn a corner. Just far enough away not to arouse Lansing's suspicion. She walked about fifty feet down the street and saw him get into a taxi. She was about to hail one for herself when she felt something sharp and metallic pressed against her back, just above her kidneys.

"Not one word," said Meisner. She didn't turn around. "We're going to do this carefully," he said. "Nod if you understand."

She nodded.

"Keep walking. If you look to the third door on your left, there's a small alleyway. Walk to the end of it. Then head to the left and up the stairs to the parking garage. You understand?"

"Do I have a choice?" she said.

"I think we're going to have a conversation about who you work for. And why you're so interested in me."

The parking garage was a three-story structure filling in the courtyard between two Gothic-style buildings. Nearly the entire floor was filled with Fiat 500s. With the occasional Renault or BMW. It was hard to find Meisner's car. He drove an ordinary grey 7-series sedan. Bland and businesslike. Kiki walked passed it before he yelled at her to halt.

"Now, what's this? On your back? What kind of equipment do you carry with you?"

Meisner's bodyguard ripped the bag off and opened it. The first thing he pulled out was her bikini top. "So," said Kiki, "anything else you want? Maybe you'd like to try it on? It might look good on you," she said to the muscled enforcer. "After the figure you've developed from all the steroids."

The guard reached forward and was about to throttle her when Meisner raised his hand. "No. We take her back to the garage. That's how we'll deal with her. We're the nicest people in the world, you know," Meisner said to her. "I hope you won't do anything that me and Franz will regret later."

A grin appeared on Kiki's face. "Oh, I understand perfectly. You're really ruining my vacation. Only this morning someone tried to steal that very bag you're holding."

Kiki remembered something that Shapiro had told her during weapons training. If you don't have a gun, you can always improvise.

As long as your target isn't moving.

Franz opened the door to the driver's side. He sat down, put on his seat belt, and then decided to unlock the doors to the back seat. All of these things Kiki made sure to note.

Meisner opened the back passenger-side door. He gripped her neck. She winced at the pain as he pushed her down into the seat. As she lowered herself inside she saw a crowbar—on the shelf behind the back seat. This was something that would normally escape one's notice, since the BMW 7-series had two prominent head rests in the back for additional passenger comfort. It had clearly been left there by accident.

She reached in and grabbed the tire iron. Swung it at his face. She missed, but it was only to distract his attention. Bracing herself she kicked backwards, landing a blow to Meisner's kneecap with the spike of her stiletto heel. As Meisner flew back, Franz took his place. She raised the crowbar again and smashed the bodyguard in the head. Meisner tried to reach in and grab her weapon. She smashed the window and proceeded to claw at the skin on Meisner's left forearm. She only scratched him superficially, but he recoiled in pain.

"What have you done, you nasty little American freak."

"Oh, I'm a freak, am I?"

WHAM!

The tire iron made contact with his jaw. The force of the blow flung him against a nearby Fiat. Kiki kicked off her heels and ran to the nearest exit.

Jesus, this was painful. She emerged onto a cobblestone street. After a few steps it was obvious that she couldn't go on like this. The sting of her soles became unbearable. What had she been thinking wearing heels? Tatyana was rubbing off on her. There was no way she could possibly escape at this speed.

Upstairs Meisner and his guard were starting to recover. With Kiki slowed down, they would catch up in minutes. She turned a corner and found herself inside a small little alleyway filled with cafes. A few doors down she found a store selling knickknacks.

She ran to the woman at the counter. "Sandals? Do you have any sandals?"

The woman looked at her blankly. "I don't speak English."

"My feet—" she pointed down.

"Ahh..." The woman smiled and gestured to the back of the store. Next to a shelf of fruit baskets was a small section devoted to beach wear. Kiki paid ten Euros for a cheap pair of flip-flops.

She ran out of the store and turned the

corner, back onto the Grand Via, right in front of the University. In front of her were thousands of people, all yelling and chanting in the biggest street protest she had ever seen.

CHAPTER 3.3

Kiki looked around. People were dressed in black hoodies and Guy Fawks masks. The whole thing was pandemonium.

SMASH!

Someone tossed a garbage can into a bank window. Perfect, she thought. They'll never find me in the middle of this. She snuggled into the crowd and found herself next to a group of naked lesbians marching with anticapitalist banners. The crowd was getting closer to a line of masked riot police.

The next thing she knew the entire protest had come to a stop. From the police side there were bullhorns shouting instructions in Spanish. To her left a line of policemen surrounded the lesbians. Somewhere behind her, people started throwing rocks at the masked officers.

BOOM!

A tear gas grenade exploded off to her

left. The crowd was devolving into chaos. The smoke drifted towards Kiki, stinging her eyes. People started running back the way they came to escape the tear gas.

The next thing she knew she was facing Meisner. He grabbed her arms and held on, dragging her towards the sidewalk.

"We're going to take you and see what that crow bar does to your body," shouted Meisner, barely audible over the screams of the protesters. His ear had a trickle of blood running down it.

Franz, the bodyguard, caught up to them. He grabbed Kiki's left arm. This time, they were going to make sure she didn't get away.

But the crowd had swallowed them up. There was no way to push through—they had to follow the mass of people. There was a resurgence of energy and again rocks were thrown at the police.

They must have been in the densest, most aggressive part of the march. Kiki looked around. They were surrounded by figures in black, faces obscured by black scarves. Great, she thought, we've stumbled into a crowd of anarchists. Meisner had made the unfortunate choice that morning of wearing a suit and tie.

The crowd abruptly changed direction,

heading back towards the parking garage from where Kiki had fled. There were shouts of "Capitalisto" and several of the anarchists slammed into Meisner. His suit was getting torn.

Next thing she knew, Kiki was facing a police officer riding an enormous horse. He was bearing down on the anarchists with a baton. Franz the bodyguard wasn't paying attention to his left side. The horse collided with him, and three other black hoods.

Kiki turned away for just a moment. When she looked back she saw Franz lying on the ground. A hoof came down right on top of him, right on his rib cage. That's going to hurt tomorrow, she thought.

Meisner was fighting off anarchists on one side, while to his right the police were kettleing more black masks toward him. Kiki smacked her foot into the side of his calf, a blow blunted by the rubber flip flop. But it was enough to get him to loosen his grip on her.

She managed to run away. Then realized she was actually around the corner from her hotel. As she entered the lobby she thought she might be safe, until she saw Meisner and the bodyguard limping toward the hotel. Franz pointed in her direction.

What was the correct plan of escape? She couldn't go to her room. The elevators were slow, they'd know where she was immediately.

So instead she walked into Tiffany's.

CHAPTER 3.4

Kiki was making a bet. She figured that Meisner and his bodyguard might shoot her on the steps of the Mandarin Oriental Hotel. But not under the watchful gaze of shop attendants. Outside there might be a car or something else they could get behind to avoid the view of witnesses or security cameras. Tiffany's was her best choice. The luxury retailer was on the first floor of the hotel. It would have cameras at every possible angle and a squad of security guards. And she could make a quick escape—the store had street access.

They might simply give up. At this point there was a very good chance she wasn't even that valuable to them. It looked like the bodyguard had taken quite the hit from the hooves of the horse. She passed through a large oak archway and walked to the jewelry counter farthest from the street.

The best thing to do was to act calm and pretend she was browsing. One of the store clerks, the youngest and the skinniest woman on the staff, came up to her. Kiki guessed she was in her mid-forties.

"Is there something I could help you with, miss?" she said, glancing over Kiki's attire. She forgot she was still wearing a tight T-shirt, shorts, and flip-flops. Not the look of a person with a lot of money.

"Oh, I'm just browsing," she said. She moved as far away from the woman as possible. Out of the corner of her eye she saw Meisner and his bodyguard enter the lobby. She found a counter where she was obscured by other customers.

She approached a solemn-faced man attending a necklace display case. "Hi, is this a platinum-covered diamond necklace?" she said, indicating with her finger.

"Yes, why?" he said with more than a trickle of condescension in his voice. "Perhaps you'd be more interested in something in gold, over here."

He was about to lead her away, but Kiki stood her ground. "Oh, no. This one right here."

"Well, that is a very expensive necklace—"

"I know." She leaned in and lowered her voice. "You'd be surprised how much money my family has. Now, would you cut the b.s. and let me try it on?"

"Well, if you're going to be insistent—"

"I am. Now stop with the attitude."

The man gazed back at her. Apparently she meant business. He called a security guard over and whispered something into his ear. The guard disappeared and she was presented with the necklace on a satin pillow. "Now be very careful."

A woman in plain clothes came over and helped her put the necklace on. "There's a mirror right over here. Why don't you take a look?"

It was clear that the diamonds were gorgeous. She'd never worn $40,000 worth of diamonds before. And to think that if DeBeers hadn't been keeping them off the market they might be worthless. Two seconds later Kiki's daydreaming was cut short.

"Ah, they are beautiful, aren't they?" said Meisner. Kiki was surrounded on both sides. "Don't you agree, Franz?"

"Yes," said the bodyguard, "you should definitely buy them, darling. But why don't we do a bit more shopping first?"

"Let me get a second opinion." Kiki rushed

away. She approached the security guard by the door. "Those two men—" She indicated toward Meisner and Franz—"I think they're trying to rob the store. They have a gun. They want me to run away with this necklace on." She took it off and handed it to him.

The guard looked like he didn't know what to think.

"You'd better get the police. They're going to rob you." She bolted out to the sidewalk, crowded with tourists. Hurried away from the hotel. The best option was the subway. Only two blocks away.

She walked quickly, trying not to attract attention.

"Stop! Stop her! She's got my wallet!"

She looked back. Meisner was the one screaming. Uh-oh. He'd one-upped her in the deceit department. Bloodied and bruised, they ran towards her. She saw a line of tourists getting on a bus. Better than nothing. It was a double-decker with an open top.

She got on. But the bus driver waved away. When she tried to walk past him he started yelling the word ticket at her over and over.

"Excuse me," she said, "I have to get on."

An ancient American woman with leather-like suntanned skin turned around. "Oh," she said in a thick New Jersey accent, "You have to go and buy a ticket. From the machine."

"I don't have time."

"It's two Euros. Just two Euros."

She looked down at the woman's hands. "Can I buy that ticket from you?"

"Well..."

Kiki produced a ten-Euro note from her shorts, handing it to the woman. She ripped the ticket out of the woman's hands and moved to the back of the bus.

The bus driver waved at the old woman to get off. "Boy," she said. "Somebody's in a hurry."

As the bus departed Kiki spotted Meisner and Franz giving up, out of breath. She'd lost them for now. Then the announcement came on. The next stop was the Segratta Familia. Great, she thought. The most famous landmark in the entire city. Maybe she could sneak off at the stop after that.

The first floor of the bus was completely packed. She walked upstairs. There was only one place to sit on the open top. Not exactly a good hiding spot. She sat down behind some tourists and kept her head low.

After ten minutes being stuck in the Barcelona traffic, she took a peek over the side. Right behind them was the BMW with Meisner driving, his bodyguard in the front seat. What the hell was she going to do? The only option was to get off at the next stop and try to mingle in with the crowd.

The bus passed the park in front of the cathedral and pulled up to the front of the church. There was an announcement in English and Spanish. They would be stopped there for two minutes. Plenty of time for Meisner to hop on and take a look around. The rest of the passengers piled out the back door. Kiki followed and did her best to blend in.

She was halfway across the plaza when Meisner and his bodyguard pulled up in the BMW. Meisner indicated to Franz. "Go there. See if she's gone inside." The bus was already pulling out, so Meisner had no choice but to follow. This was her only opportunity to get away from the bodyguard.

There's no way, she thought. The plaza's too open. She had no choice but to follow the crowd inside.

CHAPTER 3.5

The crowd poured through the gates of the Segratta Familia. Kiki was overwhelmed by the size of the place. But it seemed to flow organically. Right out of the ground. It was like no cathedral she'd been to before. The crowd just stood there, looking up at the different bits of ornamentation and pillar design. A tour guide arrived and started the tour.

It was time for Kiki to get out. She glanced back through the open doors. Meisner's bodyguard was at the edge of the plaza and getting closer. She snuck behind one of the giant stone pillars that supported the ceiling of the lobby. The best place was the darkest place. As quickly as possible she moved into one of the side chapels.

She looked around for a place to hide. Maybe she could lie down on one of the pews? That was too obvious. Then she noticed there were two confessionals in a dark, out of the way alcove. It was perfect.

She moved in closer to see if any of them were occupied. Leaning against the door, she heard nothing. She opened it and went inside.

Maybe she could wait this out for a couple of hours.

She was all settled in when the doors to the confessional beside her opened and two people shuffled in.

There was a man with a thick Italian accent. "It's okay, baby. We can go in here." Kiki couldn't believe her ears. It was like he was straight out of central casting.

"I don't know," said a young woman in a thick British accent. "This is far too open, don't you think?"

"In here, in here."

"Now wait a minute, we shouldn't be going in there. What if one of the clergy comes by? It's a very bad idea, that's what I mean."

"Yeah," said the Italian, "bad idea."

"No, this is where the priest goes," she said.

Kiki heard rustling, like the woman was trying to push the man away. There was a creaking sound as someone sat down in the chair of the confessional.

"What are you doing now? I really shouldn't be doing this," said the girl.

"No problem," the man said.

The door clicked shut. The girl sounded panicked now. "What are you doing with my bra? You shouldn't be touching there. It's not polite."

"I no speaka the English," said the man.

Kiki was shocked to hear the two of them, uh, engage in activities. The woman clearly had no intention to put up a fight. Was she going to have to listen to the two of them have sex? Escape seemed like a compelling option right now. All she could hear was the sound of muffled groaning and heavy breathing and clothes dropping to the floor.

What Kiki didn't know was that Franz, Meisner's bodyguard, had spotted these two on his way in. He was pretty shocked when he saw them scurry off to the confessional. With Kiki all but forgotten, he had followed the two, albeit at a discrete distance.

Now he wanted to get a peek for himself. He walked in to the confessional next to the couple—

—and caught Kiki hiding inside. He was shocked at his good fortune. He grinned. Stepped in. Closed the door and shook his head.

Kiki looked around. There was nothing to fight him off with. Next door the couple was getting louder. There was a bang against the wall. They were so into each other, they wouldn't notice Franz knifing her or whatever else he had in mind.

Her eyes were locked in terror to Franz.

She felt around and found, of all things, a cane. Lying between the chair and the wall of the confessional. Someone must have left it there—the priest, or some old person who had felt rather spry after confessing their sins. In one motion she whacked Franz in the crotch. He muffled a painful groan. Next door the couple froze in fear.

"Did you hear that?" asked the girl.

"I hear nothing," said the Italian.

"Oh, god, somebody's in there, next door."

Unfortunately Kiki had missed Franz's less polite parts by mere centimeters. He dove for her, grasping her neck with his thick, puffy hands.

She had to do something before he broke her neck. She lowered the cane and swung it upwards with all the strength she could muster.

THWACK!

She connected just below his jaw. Franz's neck snapped back. He released his grip on her and clutched his throat. He hyperventilated for a few moments, then collapsed onto Kiki like a sack of potatoes.

Oh my god, she thought. I broke his neck.

Meanwhile the two people next door had gone quiet.

"Maybe he's gone. I think somebody who was there is gone," said the girl.

"I no speaka the English, you know, baby." They immediately resumed their activities.

Kiki felt for a pulse. He was still breathing. Still alive.

This was insane. He was unconscious. For now. She looked down at his shoes. He was wearing boots, actually. With laces. She removed them and tied him firmly to the chair. He wasn't going anywhere anytime soon. When he woke up he could scream for help, but he'd have a lot of explaining to do. She got out of the confessional. Leaving the Italian and the British girl to themselves.

She needed to find out if Meisner had come back. In all likelihood he would leave his car out front. Finding a parking spot around here would be impossible. If he'd followed the bus to the next stop, he'd know she wasn't there. By now he could be wandering around the cathedral. She had to find the highest lookout possible. The last thing she wanted to do was to have him start shooting in a public place.

She scurried around the corner and spotted a spiral staircase. She went up four flights of stairs before she found a balcony that looked off onto the front plaza. But there wasn't a clear line of sight to the street. So she went up to the next floor.

She heard footsteps. Someone was coming down from the other direction. Probably just another awestruck tourist.

She rounded a corner and right in front of her was Meisner.

CHAPTER 4.1

Kiki's first instinct was to fight. But she knew in an instant that she was at an extreme disadvantage. Meisner must be carrying a gun. She only had flip-flops, which were hardly an effective weapon. She pivoted around and rushed down the stairwell as quickly as she could.

Meisner was right behind her. At the second floor landing she felt an arm on her back. "There's no way you're getting away from me," he said.

She felt him wrapping his arms around her. His grip cut the blood supply to her head.

Kiki felt dizzy. He might even break one of her ribs. She felt herself lifted off the floor.

"What the hell are you doing?"

"You're going over the edge. That's what I'm going to do to you. You think I won't kill you here? You don't know what kind of man I am."

She flailed hopelessly. He walked her over to the railing. Treating her like a rag doll. Slowly he moved his face closer. "Now, one last chance. You tell me, who are you working for?"

"For your mother," she said. "She wants you home."

"Wrong answer," said Meisner.

Kiki did the only thing she knew and lodged her feet in one of the openings in the railing.

"You're going over," he said.

"No, I'm not." She bent her head forward. Then smacked it back against his forehead and nose. He howled in pain. She turned around. His nostrils were a bloody wreck. She grabbed his crotch and squatted down.

Using the most forceful technique she could remember from her judo instruction she lifted him backwards. She heard a scream, then howling. The next thing she knew there was a THUNK coming from below. A woman screamed.

Kiki turned around. Meisner was gone. How could this be?

Oh my god, she thought. I just flipped him right over. He must have weighed at least three times what she did. Yet, it happened. He was gone.

She examined the rest of her body. Despite the effort Meisner had made, he wasn't very effective at injuring people. The only pain was in the back of her head. Definitely a bruise.

Kiki decided that being discreet was the best way out. She walked as far away as she could and found another spiral staircase in the corner of the building. Down on the first floor of the chapel she walked past the spot where Meisner landed.

A crowd of people had gathered. "Hey," said one man, "I called the police. His legs are broken."

"Is he still breathing?" said one woman.

"He seems okay. But how the hell did he hit his nose, too?"

"He'll live."

That's just great, thought Kiki. Of all the people who land on a cold, marble floor. He gets out with just a broken leg. She stood there with the crowd for a couple of minutes, then casually wandered off.

"I know who did it. I saw all it. It was a bald man. I think. I think he was tall, too."

"Really?" said one woman.

Kiki smiled. Well, at least she wasn't one of the likely suspects. She heard police sirens in the distance. This was her cue to wander out casually.

She didn't notice a young man reading through an English language brochure. He wore shorts and a Hawaiian shirt. Perhaps the most indiscreetly attired person in the whole place. Like he'd made an effort to look like a tourist. It wasn't working out so well. He carried himself with the air of a police detective. He folded his map and followed Kiki out.

CHAPTER 4.2

"What do you mean he was going to kill you?"

"I mean," said Kiki, "he was going to throw me over the edge."

Digby sat at his desk, on the other end of the Skype connection. "You couldn't have called for help? Didn't you have a cell phone?"

"No," she said. "They grabbed me the moment I left the hotel."

"Something's not right here. It was just a coincidence that Meisner was there?" To Tatyana, "Did you see any of this?"

"No, I wasn't there. She took the day off and went to the beach. When she came back this is the story she told."

"Look," said Digby, "there's one thing you have to be careful of in your position. When someone can identify you, the first thing you should do is report in. Follow our instructions. Don't go putting yourself in the line of fire. It's not worth it. You could've died today. Now what you've done is even worse," he said. "You attracted a huge amount of media attention."

"I don't understand how," said Kiki.

"You tried to kill a man in a church. That doesn't go over well. And not any church—the most famous one in Western Europe."

"Well, these things happen. It was me or him."

"Look, from now on, you don't leave that hotel room, okay? And you stay away from these people. It's not your decision to go and chase the bad guys. It's our decision."

"Yeah," said Kiki.

"I don't care if you have to tie her up, she's not leaving that room."

Tatyana nodded, a serious look on her face. "I understand," she said.

Kiki felt uncomfortable. "Any other instructions?"

"The flight leaves tomorrow morning at ten. Be on it. You understand?"

"Got it."

Digby signed off. "Well," said Tatyana, "at least you'll get a chance to order room service."

"I think he was being unfair with me. Don't you?"

"With this incident? Obviously you haven't been getting the same e-mails I have. The committee made quite a fuss. Some of them had to be talked out of firing you. In fact, there's a rumor that one of them had a video of you being followed out of the cathedral."

"By who?"

"Probably someone from a foreign intelligence agency. Don't you realize that maybe someone else could be following us when we do one of our jobs?"

"Why would someone do that?"

"It's a spy versus spy world. What can I say?"

"Who would spy on someone like me?"

"I have no idea. But we're not affiliated with any country, you understand? We're freelance."

"That doesn't answer my question."

"We might have secrets that we keep from our individual governments. Or even stuff that the Russians have shared with us."

"I thought we were a part of NATO?"

"We are. But, you know, things can get kind of... muddled."

"What do you mean?"

"Lately there's been a lot of talk about a lot of things. Internal moles. People betraying people. Or not betraying people. Even Digby's been suspect."

"And you haven't?"

"Most people know what I'm in it for. They give me money. I do my work. And in a couple of years I'm out of here. Retire to some private island somewhere."

"With real estate prices these days?"

"The bottom line is people are getting increasingly paranoid. I don't know where this is going to end up. I'll tell you something, though, the world is going back to the way it was sixty or seventy years ago."

"What about this Meisner guy? Who is he?"

"He is like us. An independent contractor. If you had left him alone, we wouldn't have any problems, you understand?"

"Aren't we supposed to pursue the bad guys?"

"The bad guys? Think about the people that you put in the hospital today. To them, we're the bad guys. I don't know much about this guy Meisner. But I think he's just a capitalist. He's not a communist or a terrorist. He means well."

"Huh?"

"He's only in it for profit. Which is the same as most people."

"That's part of the problem," said Kiki "everybody's doing it for money now. And no one has any loyalty to anyone."

"We don't live in a perfect world. Do we?"

"Yeah, and it stinks."

"Well, it smells like money to me. Now, tomorrow—we need to be on that flight. If you try to leave this room I will tie you up. Those are my orders."

Kiki picked up the room phone. "What's the number for room service?"

CHAPTER 4.3

They had arrived in Barcelona by train, taking the high-speed line after doing some investigating in Paris. After Spain they were headed directly to Amsterdam, so they opted for the airport. Seemingly as a punishment, Digby had booked them on Polish Airlines. Notorious for discounts. And a limited track record of landing planes intact.

All the way to the airport Kiki was silent, lost in her thoughts. The previous night had given her lots of time to think. She still wondered why no one took her seriously. No matter what she did, she was treated like an impetuous schoolgirl. Sure, she was the youngest among the staff. But she resented being punished like a little child.

"You know," she told Tatyana, "the only reason I took this job was to find out who killed my grandfather. And the only reason they won't fire me is because I have files on them. Stuff they don't want leaked out. I really want to go through the boxes and find out why they keep me around. It feels like I'm in some sort of holding pattern."

"Well," said Tatyana, "They want you. But if you keep behaving like this you might get that vacation you've been asking for."

"How did you know about that?"

Tatyana just smiled.

They made their way to El Prat Airport Terminal Two. The place was old. And mostly abandoned by the major airline carriers when the more modern terminal one had been built a few years earlier. A facility with over a hundred different stores and restaurants had been reduced to a mere dozen or so. The terminal was vast. And empty.

"You could play a whole round of golf in here."

"Yes," said Tatyana. "It's not exactly the nicest way to depart Spain, is it?" They made their way to the departure counter. Only to discover one of their seats was no longer available.

"I'm terribly sorry," said the clerk. "It's just that we had a weather delay last night. There were business travelers who couldn't fly out until this morning." Tatyana argued with the woman for a few more minutes before realizing it was hopeless.

"You should go first," she said when she calmed down.

Kiki shook her head. "You go. I know you want to get back to you-know-who."

"What are you talking about?" she said.

"I know about your relationships, you know."

Tatyana glared in reply. She gave up when she saw Kiki was unfazed. "Who else knows?"

"Everyone."

A sympathetic look spread across Tatyana's face. "The next plane isn't for another six hours. You'll be stuck in this hell hole."

"I'll live. It's okay."

And so she stayed there. Waiting. With a suitcase. After an hour she found a coffee shop. Where an ill-tempered woman poured her an oversized cup of black sludge. She decided it best to hide herself behind a novel for a few hours. Maybe even take a nap.

In the third hour of her sojourn she decided to wander around the terminal. Just to see what kind of people were stuck at each gate.

And there he was. The man that Meisner had called Mr. Lansing. Sitting at the gate for a flight to Frankfurt.

CHAPTER 5.1

Kiki didn't know what to do. She knew she wasn't supposed to be following anyone. But she looked at the gate. He was traveling to Frankfurt on an AirBrussels flight.

So she phoned Digby. Four rings. Got his voicemail message. She hung up the phone. Obviously he was hung over. It was a Saturday morning.

Well, it was only to Frankfurt. That was practically on the way to Amsterdam, anyway. A little detour couldn't hurt. She went back through security and bought herself a ticket on the same flight.

An hour later they landed. She kept her eye on the guy. He was no more than three rows in front of her. They had arrived ten minutes early. But the flight was still waiting to get the clearance to deplane.

After forty-five minutes of waiting they stumbled off. Kiki and the rest of the passengers boarded a small bus. They were packed in like sardines. She could barely keep track of Lansing in the crowd. After a tight five-minute ride they were deposited at the terminal.

It took forever to wind through a labyrinth of corridors in the underbelly of Frankfurt Airport. Finally they got to the baggage carousel. There they waited for twenty-five minutes.

She noticed Lansing constantly checking his watch. He picked up his luggage and made it through the lineup for customs. Then took off in a sprint. It wasn't just him. Three other people were also trying to get away as fast as possible.

She looked back. They had gotten off at terminal two. She followed him all the way back to terminal one. He rechecked at the Air Canada gate. She looked up at the board. The next flight was to Montreal. At one-thirty. She had forty-five minutes to board. That should be plenty of time. She went to the booking agent.

"I'm sorry. Could you help me? I just have to go to Montreal on the next flight."

The check-in clerk eyed her warily. "I'm sorry, but there is barely enough time. There's a good chance you won't make it."

"You don't understand. A member of my family has died and I've got to be there right now."

The clerk clicked through her computer. "We can put you on a flight to Halifax at three."

Kiki put on hysterics. "I have to be on the next flight to Montreal. It's complicated." She covered her face. "It's a suicide watch." She was really pulling this one out of her ass.

"What?"

"I don't really want to talk about it." She was only going to go so far with this performance.

"Well, I can't guarantee you'll make the flight—"

"But it's in forty-five minutes. I'm already in the right terminal, aren't I?" said Kiki.

"But the time to get through security—"

"I'll risk it." After paying an extraordinary sum for the ticket, she checked her luggage. The next step was to get through security. No mean feat. She saw the lineup. It was stopped. There was a fast line, but she was quickly shuffled aside by the security guard when she presented her ticket.

"Not here," he said in a brusque German voice, gesturing to the regular line.

Another twenty minutes passed before she slowly moved to the head of the queue. She took off her shoes and was patted down by snickering security guards. After the all clear she picked up her carry-on bag and headed to the gate for her flight.

She looked up at the departure board. Gate A31. But after turning a corner she was greeted by two completely different directions.

Schengen?

Non-Schengen?

Kiki was in trouble. None of the gates were indicated in any way a reasonable person could understand. This could mean going through another set of passport controls. She walked up to the nearest airport employee.

"I can't help you," said the woman. "I'm really sorry."

"Just tell me where Gate A31 is." She glared at the woman. "Please, my flight leaves in twenty minutes."

Reluctantly the woman examined the ticket. "Well, you have to go out to the Schengen Zone."

"So I have to go through another gate?"

"I'm afraid so."

Desperation was kicking in. She understood now why Lansing had been running. Finally she found a second passport control office. It was closed. She hustled to the other side of the terminal. Finally finding an open desk.

"Okay, here you go," the man said politely. "But I don't think you're going to make it."

"Why not? What do you mean?"

"Well, there's a bus."

"A bus?"

"That gate is just a loading point."

Kiki sprinted as fast as she could go. She passed gate after gate, weaving between weary travelers. For at least half a kilometer. She glanced over and saw both moving sidewalks were working. Both in the opposite direction. Finally she arrived at the gate.

"Hold the plane!"

"No," said the nearest flight attendant, "this gate has already closed—"

She ran past her. Through the doorway and down a flight of stairs. She saw the bus, about to pull out. She ran up and alongside it. Banging on the side window. The bus driver saw her and opened the door. "You can't come on. It's too dangerous."

"But I'm here," she said.

"Fine." She stepped on and everybody applauded.

This was a disaster, she thought. Now he'll know exactly what I look like.

Nine hours later the plane landed. She found her way through the Montreal airport. Lansing was waiting at a gate for a flight to Quebec City. It left in three hours.

While she watched him, her phone rang. It was Digby.

"Kiki, what the hell's going on?" He was pissed.

"This may need some explaining to do."

"What you mean? Are you coming into the office tomorrow? We can go through this in the debriefing."

"I'm not exactly nearby."

"Where are you?"

"In Montreal."

CHAPTER 5.2

"You're giving me a cigarette case?"

"This," said Tin Man, "is the most important piece of equipment we've developed in the past five years."

Digby shook his head. "An exploding cigarette?"

"The idea came from an old James Bond movie." Tin Man raised the stick of tobacco in front of Digby's face. "This cigarette could save your life."

Digby stroked the gunmetal case he'd been given. A floral pattern had been engraved on its surface. "Interesting." He opened it. Examined the contents. "But I don't smoke Marlboroughs."

"You don't put your own cigarettes in it," said Tin Man. "Those four were manufactured by us. As ammunition."

Digby wasn't impressed. "I'm supposed to open my pack. Hand over one of my cigarettes. And then what?"

"Once the opponent has the cigarette, all they have to do is light it, and it will explode."

"And what if they don't? Maybe they notice that something's up?"

Tin Man brandished the cigarette case. He stroked the edge, near the clasp. "You see this? The latch, on the side here? You pull it down and to the right. This activates the remote control."

Digby fingered the small piece of metal. Felt it click into place. "Okay."

"Now," said Tin Man, "in the gun metal

case we've embedded a miniature transmitter."

"Got it," said Digby, about to clasp the holder closed.

"Wait—"

Digby stopped dead.

"Don't shut it. That's what causes the remote to activate. It will detonate any cigarette left outside the case. A big cloud of tear gas. And it doesn't just shoot out of the tip. It also goes backwards, too. If someone is holding the fag, there is no way it won't go off in an opponent's face."

Digby smiled. "What a lovely British turn of phrase."

"Huh?"

"Nothing."

"In the tests, the gas cloud was effective for about twenty-five seconds. Incapacitates a normal person."

"Well," said Digby, "that's just great. Now, in our modern age, all I need to find is a person who smokes cigarettes. Who happens to have run out. And smokes my brand. And is willing to accept one from me, a man of dubious character. Did the lab calculate the chances of all those things occurring in a crisis situation?"

"Well, you could leave one on a table for the victim. Surely a dedicated non-smoker will become curious at the sight of a cigarette on their desk, right?"

"Or maybe you could build me a rifle. Hidden in a buggy whip?" Digby stood up. Surveyed the metal table where various pieces of dismembered electronics and computers were sprawled out. Tin Man had cleaned up since the last time he'd been here. The lava lamps still held court on every available flat surface, but his decor was going through a Moroccan phase. His bed and the floor were covered with pillows and throws acquired on a recent trip to the Maghreb.

Something caught Digby's eye. He looked out to the Task Force Ten conference area. Lisl and Tatyana had arrived. He left Tin Man at his desk to say hello. "So what's the deal? Have you tracked her down?"

"Yes," said Lisl. "Jenny and Mei are still in Boston. They've tried Phillips-Exeter and Litchfield. But they've found nothing resembling the academy connection."

"How many more places are they going to visit?"

"They think two more weeks in New England."

Digby shook his head. "This is ridiculous. The trail's run completely cold." He sighed. "Kiki's nearby, right?"

Lisl nodded. "I need time to make a plan."

"You do that. But hurry up."

Lisl disappeared upstairs to her office. Tatyana sat on the couch, concentrating on her phone. Digby grabbed a chair from the conference table. Sat down across from her. "Okay," he said, "you're supposed to be the senior leader—"

"What is this, an interrogation?" She stroked her blond hair. "I am not a babysitter."

"I don't care," said Digby. "She's been working here less than three months. You could try a little harder to keep things on track."

"I kept her locked in the hotel room. That was all you asked of me. I am not here to supervise a twenty-two year old." Tatyana leaned forward. "Next time, if you want things to go smoothly, don't ask Lisl to book us on a discount flight. This organization has become, as you say in English, penny wise and dollar foolish."

Digby leaned back on his chair. "To be honest, I don't care how you guys spend money. For me, every day I spend at Task Force Ten is a day I can't focus on other problems. I have five hundred agents to co-ordinate throughout Europe. All with coded transmissions to give and orders to receive.

Four hundred different drops are happening over the next five weeks. Just tell me I don't need to worry about what's going on down here, okay?"

"Well," she said, "we do important stuff."

"But only in Europe. That's our mandate. Does Kiki even know we don't operate in other countries?"

Tatyana just smiled.

CHAPTER 5.3

"We found out where he is," said Lisl.

"And? What's the deal?"

"Well, just make sure you're very, very careful. You're on your own over there, you know."

"Fine, fine, I get that. Right now the subject is out of sight. I'd like to know where he might end up."

"He's staying at the Chateau Frontenac."

"That's expensive. Downtown?"

"That's the one."

"Will you reimburse me for this?"

"We'll think about it," said Digby in the background

"I'm sure you won't have to worry about

money," said Lisl. "Do you need instructions on how to get there?"

"It's alright," said Kiki. "I've been before. When I was a child."

The cab ride took forever. Quebec City was in the middle of a summer festival. All over town tourists had taken over. Not just from other parts of Canada and the northeastern United States, but also from Europe.

The taxicab meandered through the streets of the old city. It had been ages since she'd been here. Kiki was mesmerized by the ancient stone buildings. The fact that in North America much of a city could be over four hundred years old.

As she left the Airport she felt a bit of culture shock. She hadn't been back to North America in a while. Somehow, in her heart of hearts, she missed the suburban four lane roads with their doughnut shacks and gas stations. Endless discount stores. But now she was back on cobblestone streets. Even far narrower and less organized than those of Barcelona.

The taxi headed off the highway, to the narrow streets of old Quebec City. Kiki took the opportunity to shut her eyes. When she awoke from her brief nap they were pulling into the courtyard of the Chateau Frontenac.

The place had the look of a Transylvanian castle. It was amazing. A doorman arrived to take her baggage.

"Will you take it up to my room?"

"Of course, mademoiselle."

She saw Lansing at the check-in counter. He'd arrived only moments before.

"I'll be okay," he said to the bellhop.

She took out her cell phone and plugged in a set of headphones. It looked like she was simply playing an ordinary video game. But in fact it was a sophisticated eavesdropping program. With a shotgun microphone at the front edge of the phone. She was able to aim it directly at the clerk standing next to Lansing.

"Easy. I don't speak any French."

"It won't be a problem here, sir. But go outside of the hotel it's very difficult to find people who speak English. But in most restaurants you shouldn't have any problems."

"Great. The ferry to Levis—how often does it run?"

The woman was puzzled. "You want to go to Levis?"

Lansing just stared at her for a moment. "Do you have a ferry schedule?"

"Yes, of course we do."

"I'm meeting a relative tonight."

"Sure, here is the schedule. And here is the key to 1701."

"Very good. Thank you very much."

"If there's anything else we can do for you, sir?"

"No, not for now."

Kiki felt bad that he had not tipped the bellhop. Obviously the man needed to make a living. Lansing didn't know what the hell to do when the attendant approached. Nothing had destroyed a bellhop's livelihood more than the person who invented wheels on a suitcase.

She checked in immediately. "It's okay. You can just give me the key."

"Can you sign here?" The women looked at her with bit of cynicism. She was still wearing her T-shirt, shorts, and flip-flops.

"Sure." Kiki took the pen. "Is there a department store around here that sells women's clothing?"

"Right around the corner, ma'am."

CHAPTER 6.1

Kiki was staying on the fourth floor. She looked around the elegantly appointed hotel room. It had a fantastic view of the St. Lawrence, and of old Quebec. They'd even left a few chocolates and a bathrobe on her pillow. This place was not half bad. It even had poutine on the room service menu. She'd definitely have to take advantage of that before she left.

She opened her suitcase and grabbed a small satchel filled with different devices. Pulled out a small card. It looked like something you would get from a cell phone provider. She popped out a green SIM card from plastic molding.

Then she went up to 1701. She glanced down the hall. Was anybody around? No. She listened carefully through the door. It sounded like Lansing was in the shower. She took out the green SIM. With an innocuous piece of green tape she stuck it against the lip of the wood molding around the doorframe. Out of sight from someone approaching the room. It was small enough that it would take a proper search to find it. She went back to the area by the elevators and checked her phone.

It was working. It would tell her when Lansing decided to open the door and head out.

CHAPTER 6.2

The Communication Surveillance Department at NATO Special Services occupied the largest space in the building. It must have been a ballroom in decades past. Digby had been told the room was perhaps the largest in all of Amsterdam. And right now it was packed, wall-to-wall, with antiquated communications equipment.

"This is how you do signals intelligence these days?" said Digby to one of the white-coated technicians nearby.

"Excuse me?" said the tech, taking off his headphones.

"Nothing," said Digby. He wandered over to the other side of the room.

Tin Man was sitting at a table with a frighteningly low-tech spread of papers and pencils. He turned to Digby and handed him a pad of paper. On it were printed what looked like word-search puzzles. "Do you know what these are?"

"Of course I do. It's a one time pad."

"Amazing, isn't it?" said Tin Man. "Each of these numbers on the top corresponds to a code. And you only use it once to send a message. So basically A equals G. And B equals R. Along with other numbers and symbols. Each sheet at the top has a number, with a different way of translating the code." Tin Man pointed to the corner of the pad. "You're looking at sheet number twenty-two. When someone sends you a secret letter, you'd use only that sheet to decode it."

Digby looked at him. How could something so simple be such a novelty to Tin Man? After working in a spy agency for years? Clearly he knew very little about tradecraft. "It isn't nineteen sixty-five, you know."

"Yes, but this is the most foolproof method ever developed to encode messages. Even our most powerful supercomputers can't crack it."

"But the problem is," said Digby, "both people need a copy of the one-time pad. If you lose your copy, that's the end of the story. And then there's the issue of how you send the coded messages."

"Ah, yes," said Tin Man. He reached over and grabbed a plastic freezer bag of white shoelaces. Tin Man held one up. "An ordinary shoelace, for a pair of trainers."

"Trainers?" said Digby. "You mean, sneakers?"

"Exactly. You take the lace, place it in a bowl of milk. For about ten minutes. Then the message shows up along the side of it. In black letters."

Digby grabbed the lace and examined it. "And how do you erase the message?

"Ten minutes. In a bowl filled with vinegar and water." Tin Man grabbed the lace from Digby. "In the tips are wireless receivers. We send an agent a message on their phone. It's received on the shoelace."

"And we're going through this complication because...?"

"So if a third party intercepts it, they won't think to examine the carrier data. They'll look at the message and dismiss it. Unless they're trained in our methods."

Digby checked his watch. "I think the lunch hour's over. I have to get back."

"Give 'em hell," said Tin Man.

"Are you heading back to Task Force headquarters?"

"Not yet. I want to have a look at this old equipment. See if there's anything I can work with. The Chinese will never expect us to use machines from the nineteen seventies."

Digby said goodbye and got up. He navigated his way through tables filled with old electronics and ancient machines used for code breaking. He zigzagged his way to the giant double-oak doors that opened onto the hallway leading to the committee room.

While the building was ancient, the committee room was ultra modern. Sound and signal-proof. It had to be, given the discussions that went on there. The walls were a metallic grey. The lighting, low. Each delegate, representing a founding member of NATO, plus Germany, had a desk with a nameplate and a light. Their faces were shrouded in shadow. The best way to keep them from becoming a target for non-aligned security agencies. If someone snuck in a camera, it would be difficult to make a decent recording. The light level was too low.

Digby took the center seat. It was like a witness stand right in the middle of the cavernous room. After a few words of banter the rest of the committee members took their seats. The meeting was being chaired by the French delegate. "So," she said, "we were on the topic concerning the Peruvians when we broke for lunch."

Digby nodded. "But I think that's a bit premature, though. We have a better lead in Canada."

"Why would there be spies there?" asked the U.K. delegate, speaking before the light on his nameplate came on.

Digby looked around. The Canadian delegate was absent. "Every country has spies, sir. This is a very good lead."

"But signals intelligence—"

"Is completely useless," finished Digby. "Unless a crime has already been committed. I'm in the business of stopping terrorist attacks. Not playing detective after the fact. That means I use humans. On the ground. They make mistakes, but they're much better at finding perpetrators. And keeping an eye on them. Rather than spending a year decoding cryptic text messages."

"That's all very well," said the German delegate, "but how much is this going to cost?

Not just in money, but in risking our reputation? The mandate of Task Force Ten, and most of the agents under your umbrella, is in western Europe."

"It's the cost of doing business," said Digby.

"You're spending a hundred percent of your yearly budget in the next three weeks."

Digby shrugged. "If the NATO governments had spent more on nuclear security, I wouldn't have to ask for this money. If you like, I can take my agents and put them back translating e-mails."

The German shook his head. "We've learned quite a bit from the data we've put together—"

"You know nothing," said Digby. "With my highest deference and respect to your claim." He leaned forward. "Don't get too excited with what some twenty-two year old computer nerd over in Cheltenham has pulled out of his ass. These people are on to our scams. They have been for years. But you're still acting like you've got all the cards. While you sit at the table with your pants draped around your ankles. If only your boffins had been a bit less greedy, we wouldn't be in this boat. Now you're stuck with me. Are there people in your individual countries with better skills than my group? Possibly. But we've got the head start on this. And we've been pissed on by someone we trusted."

Silence hung in the room for a moment. "Very well," said the German. "Your point is well taken. What will be your next step?"

Digby sat back in the chair. Surveyed the group in the shadows. He had no idea what Kiki was up to. Until Lisl showed him a plan, he had nothing to tell them. "For the sake of security, I'm afraid I can't discuss it. Just trust me on this."

CHAPTER 6.3

Hours later Kiki was awoken by the alarm from her cell phone. Lansing was on the move. She was exhausted from the jet lag. At first it was a struggle to get going. The thought of him meeting Ridley popped into her head like a bolt of electricity. She got moving.

She grabbed her bag and was out of the room in less than a minute. What if she saw Lansing in the lobby? Three times in two days was a bit too much of a coincidence. She had to be careful. It wouldn't be hard to check if somebody was following him. Canada was not a good place to disappear in a crowd.

Kiki looked around the lobby, but didn't see Lansing. Not until she emerged in the courtyard in front of the main entrance. She looked to her left and caught sight of a man in a white dress jacket and a Panama hat. Could that be him? He walked around to the rear of the hotel, across from a park. The area was mostly deserted. Kiki kept back for a few moments. One glance over his shoulder and he would catch sight of her. She lingered in the short tunnel that connected the courtyard to the street for a minute or two, then continued on. Lasing had already strolled out onto the large piazza that surrounded the hotel. All around her the square was packed with tourists. There were buskers and food stands set up. Perfect for keeping Kiki's pursuit obscured.

Despite the mass of people, she never lost sight of the Panama hat. It was heading for the edge of the square. Toward the lookoff. Over the St. Lawrence River. It was so obvious where Lansing was headed. It was like he'd made an effort to attract the attention of the authorities. Was this all part of the plan discussed in that Barcelona restaurant?

The square was crowded with tables. Some set up for games, others for street food from local restaurants. She held back as Lansing stopped at a table that served poutine with maple syrup. Kiki moved in closer, trying to eavesdrop on his conversation. He kept trying to ask about the menu. But the two middle-aged women running the table were unable to respond in English. Unbelievable, she thought. They sent him all this way with a complete lack of linguistic ability. For all you know he might not even make it to the rendezvous.

Closer to the lookoff the crowds got thicker. Kiki found herself surrounded by buskers. People in costumes. Clowns. Children laughing. This was quite the turnout. She had no idea what was going on until she noticed some writing on a balloon. It was some sort of civic anniversary. That made sense. The city was over four hundred years old.

"Hey Kiki!"

She turned and faced a young man staring at her.

"Kiki! Don't you remember me?"

Her mind drew a blank. She had no idea who this guy was.

"You know, from McGill. From the Plateau."

"Yes," she said suspiciously.

"Don't you remember? I used to pop by your apartment from time to time. With your roommate, Suzanne."

"Your name is Rod—"

"Derek. Derek Macintosh. You don't remember now?"

"No, I had no idea—"

"It's so good to see you. What are you up to these days?"

"I'm actually late for an appointment."

"It's very nice to see you. Have you spoken to Suzanne lately?"

"No, I haven't."

"I know," he said. "We really weren't that close."

"Well, I have to go now. Bye. She walked away briskly."

That was awkward, Kiki thought. She had no idea who he was. A guest from one of those nights where alcohol had clouded her memory.

The man watched her walk away for a few moments. He would continue his pursuit. Later. His name was Hawthorne Steele and he had been tracking her all the way from the Segratta Familia. Tonight he was working for the CIA.

He grabbed his cell phone. "Hey, it's me. I've confirmed the name you gave me. Are we moving on to phase two?" The response didn't make him happy. "Why? You brought me all the way here."

Steele was disappointed. He really wanted

to see an arrest happen. He could use it on his otherwise thin C.V. This girl was obviously nothing but trouble. How many people were going to die tonight because of her?

Kiki wandered around the lookoff. She caught sight of Lansing on the other side of the square. Heading into a building marked 'Funicular'. She struggled to get through the crowds.

Inside Kiki faced a line of people. The 'Funicular' was some sort of railway, that connected the square by the hotel to the streets below. She arrived just in time to see a train car depart, with Lansing on board.

Kiki cursed the man who ran into her. She had no idea who he was. But the guy really managed to bungle her pursuit. Glumly she lined up for the next train.

CHAPTER 6.4

Ridley had gone into town. A place called Senneterre. It was tiny. As far as he could tell this was the end of the line. It was a rail town with a few stores and a small army garrison. He found himself at the local Co-op, trying to figure out signage that was all in French. He came upon, of all things, in the middle of the meat aisle, moose meat steak.

"Excuse me," he said to the woman at the meat counter.

She looked at him blankly. "I don't speak English," she said to him in French.

Over the past twenty-four hours Ridley had become acutely aware that he was on his own. Both physically and emotionally. Concerned no one was updating him on the situation with the police. It wasn't as if this was a small time operation, like a bank robbery. He was the linchpin. Everything at this location had rested on him. He worried how much longer he would be valuable to these people. He'd done this for the money and for the revenge. But the truth was, in a few days from now his role would be finished. They could simply wipe their hands of him. Of course they would lose half the money they paid. Since it was already in his account in Antigua.

That was the one image that kept him going. He had decided to move to Grenada. He had a place all picked out. A small village near Gouyave. He'd be there on the beach. Touristy. But still not the main stop for every cruise ship. He could banter with the locals. While they complain about other foreigners coming in just for the booze and the sun. And let them worry about things like economic development. While he sat on a boat. Fishing and hiking. Sitting in the sun. Being bored while he hid from authorities.

He was still feeling bad about leaving Kiki behind. Part of him wasn't lying when he told her he really had feelings for her. But she was so naive. Rich and set up for everything in life. Nothing like that would happen to him.

Not for someone who grew up in east London, a poor, mixed race council tenant kid. That neither his Iranian mother nor his white father were willing to acknowledge was fully part of their culture. His parents got divorced at such a young age. His happiest memories were always of his grandparents. That was the one thing that he and Kiki shared in common. They both couldn't handle their immediate family.

Now neither of their grandparents were alive. They had shared their feelings of being alone in the world. The night before he had dreamed of her. Her body lying next to his. Naked. The first thing he was going to do when this was all over was find a nice Caribbean whore. If he couldn't get it for free. He would have enough money. No more worries about things like that ever again.

He decided on the moose meat for dinner.

And bought some potatoes. A pack of cigarettes. He didn't like to smoke. It was a dirty habit. But given the way his nerves would be, it would give him something to do over the next few hours. While he waited for the person who was his contact. A man named Zebra.

Of course, Zebra was just his code name. Ridley had no idea who this guy really was. He suspected he wasn't one of the Germans, but one of the Brazilians. This thing was a mixed bag of nationalities—Swedes, Germans, Brazilians, Peruvians, Carribbeans. Was this the future in the fight against the American Empire? And to tell you the truth he still had no idea who was paying his salary.

He drove back to the mine before the sun came down. Took a few false turns intentionally. Made a loop around the area. Just to avoid being followed. But in the end he needn't have bothered. The roads stayed empty his entire journey back.

At the mine he saw a white Cadillac Escalade parked outside the warehouse. He hoped this was who he though it was. To the right of the hangar door there stood a man wearing a Zebra hair jacket.

"A bit obvious don't you think?" said Ridley as he hopped out of his truck.

"I like to blend in with the working classes," said The Zebra. "These are my two guards—Mr. T and Mr. W." They exchanged greetings. "They'll be assisting us for the time being."

"Really?" said Ridley. "They're not going to cause any trouble, are they? I don't want any yahoos on this operation. We don't need thugs who shoot their guns off at everything that twitches in a three mile radius."

"They are two of the finest Belarusian agents you are going to find."

"How did you get through the border?"

"That was not a problem. Tourists going hunting. These boys here—they only need a twenty-two and a thirty-odd six. A couple shotguns. And a couple other Smith and Wesson special nine millimeters. Unfortunate we couldn't get any assault rifles. Everything in this country has to be smuggled in from Buffalo."

"Where do you want to begin?"

"Maybe you should debrief us."

"There isn't much more to say. A cop comes in and pulled up to the hangar. Didn't look inside. Haven't seen them since." Ridley unlocked the door.

"We managed to get a copy of the police report. They figured it was some sort of model airplane that came down in the sky."

"That's it?" he said. "A model airplane? He didn't see me attached to the back?"

"Apparently not. If he did, he must have thought it was some sort of gag."

"I want those guys to sleep outside. In the truck."

"They'll sleep inside with the rest of us."

"This place has only one bathroom, you know that?"

"I know."

The Zebra entered the hangar and gazed in awe at the Daedalus. "What a magnificent piece of work." He walked over to the plane and touched it, stroking his hand over the smooth metal contours. "To think they spent five billion dollars to manufacture this. They made the perfect weapon. And they didn't even put ammunition in it."

"Well, that's the question, isn't it? Whether we can load it with the bomb."

"You need not be concerned."

Ridley wasn't convinced. "This is a prototype, you know. The first one. As in, we don't know if anything will work."

"When this is all over you'll be a very rich man. You have nothing to complain about."

Ridley kept quiet. The Zebra was pissing him off. Eventually he broke his silence.

"Where is the technician? And the device?"

The Zebra led him outside. Opened the back of the Cadillac.

"That's it?" said Ridley, looking at the box. It looked like it was built to hold ice skates. "That was what I smuggled out?"

"The device itself is small. They've really come a long way since the 1940's. Increasing the destructive power. It's actually quite heavy. The actual nuclear warhead is only the size of a golf ball. But even that could take out a city of eight million people."

"Will take out," said Ridley. "I thought that was the plan."

CHAPTER 6.5

The sun was setting on Quebec City. It was staggeringly beautiful, watching the stone buildings illuminated by the final rays of sunshine for the day.

But Kiki was enjoying none of it. She had been wandering around for forty-five minutes. Circling around the old city to the ferry termi-nal. Since she'd got off the Funicular, she'd lost sight of Lansing. It was eight-thirty and she was starving. She couldn't go on like this.

Kiki realized she'd made a really bad decision to try this on her own. The golden rule for surveillance was strength in numbers. One person really wasn't enough. She'd go back to Amsterdam, explain to Digby. Getting treated like an adult would have to be put off a little while longer.

She wandered into the only restaurant that wasn't completely packed. The Bistrot Pape-Georges. It looked expensive, but there was nothing else on the street but stores for women's clothing. French was her third language, but it didn't take much effort to order a salad. With fresh salmon. And mineral water. She'd go back to doing what she did the night before. Sitting it out in her hotel room.

She was munching her way through the salad when she spotted Lansing. Darting into the store across the street. Well, she thought, maybe my instincts aren't so bad after all. Why would he need to browse for designer dresses? she wondered. She scarfed down a few final bits of spinach. Lansing emerged from the boutique. Headed down the street. Kiki stood up, leaving a twenty-dollar bill at the table. That's one helluva a tip, she thought. It doesn't matter. She had to get going.

Lansing followed a zigzag pattern. All

through old Quebec City. He had to know that she was following him. This was a classic pattern to avoid foot surveillance.

He went in and out of the same door three times. Fortunately Kiki had dark hair. Nice and innocuous. Just like most of the people in the crowd clogging the narrow street that led to the harbor. The only convenient thing about having mixed Asian features. She looked like three quarters of the world's population.

Finally Lansing ended the chase and made for the ferry. It was a total nightmare to get on. It had just docked. Crowds and cars piled out of it. A huge lineup to get on went all the way around the block. Then Kiki saw a sign in French. Usually the ferry went directly from Quebec City across the river to Levis. This is where people could catch the train going to Montreal and eastern Canada.

Tonight, though, was a special cruise. For the street festival, there was a light show stretching on an enormous wire from the old port lands. Right across the mouth of the river where it narrowed. It was the follow-up work by a Quebec movie director named Robert Cormier. Some sort of video presentation.

The boat departed. The sun was down. Everything went dark. The ferry crew turned down the lights. An announcement came on. "The video would be lighting up the river-bank to the right. Please be careful in the low lighting. Lights will return to normal once the presentation is finished."

Kiki heard a man talking to his girlfriend, right behind her. "This was a work of art," he said in casual Quebec French. "Like a video art version of fireworks. There had been talks of taking it on tour. To Shanghai. And Hong Kong."

The ferry set off, heading up the river. A slow cruise northeast, along the coast. They're all here for the show. Kiki looked around. Once again she lost sight of Lansing.

Then she noticed a face turned away from the water. Staring at her. It was him. Her cover was blown. What's the worst thing I could do? she wondered. So she walked over and stood next to him.

"You've been following me, haven't you?" he said.

"What gives you that idea?"

CHAPTER 7.1

"I'm assuming that's why you did all that fancy footwork. Trying to avoid me," she said.

"Well, you have a nasty habit of showing up everywhere I go. This is the third time. Is it not?"

"Tell me, can I be honest with you?" said Kiki.

"Sure, but—are you a cop?"

"No. More like a freelancer. Let's just say I was hired to keep an eye on things. You have a reputation for being somewhat unreliable." It was a wild guess. Kiki had no idea who the guy was. It seemed to jive with what she heard in the Barcelona restaurant.

Lansing chuckled. "Another person who

thinks I'm unreliable. Well, I am. What are you going to do about it?"

Kiki moved closer. "I'm not going to do anything." She stroked his arm, running her fingers down his white sleeve. "Maybe you could tell me a bit more about Meisner's friends." She moved towards his stomach and danced her fingers around his upper thigh.

Her eyelids fluttered as she met his gaze. The guy must have been pushing fifty. He honestly believed she was interested in him? Whatever happened, no one could deny he was criminally stupid.

Kiki walked away. To the right side of the boat. The other passengers had moved to the port side. It had the best view of the video art display. A giant light show started, displayed on the walls of grain silos. And a giant net stretched all the way out along the banks of the Saint Lawrence River.

It was staggering in its brightness and color. Kiki was amazed how it lit up the entire boat like daylight. Except for the starboard side. She beckoned to Lansing, and walked to a dark corner. He followed her. The guy couldn't complete a simple task without getting distracted by a girl. Even though he wasn't very good looking. She guessed he wasn't married.

He came over. The first thing he did was try to grope her left breast and kiss her.

She pushed him back. "What's all this stuff?" He was carrying a soft brown leather pouch. "Take off your coat." She poked at the pouch. "What is this? Your laptop case?" Kiki opened it up. "What's inside here? Looks heavy."

"It's important stuff."

"Put it down," she instructed.

"I think you're really beautiful," he said as he dropped the bag on the deck.

"You're really old," she said, pushing against him.

"This is a great opportunity," he said. "You coming over to talk to me. An inspiration." He moved in and kissed her deep. She felt his tongue squishing about. Her mouth clenched tight and pulled back. Yuck. This man is a thousand years old. He hadn't even bothered to shave.

"Now back off," she said, and pushed him away.

"What do you mean?" he said. "You're my little prize."

"I'm nobody's prize." She punched him square in the stomach.

"You little bitch. I'll show you. Right over the side."

BANG! SMACK!

She whacked him hard. Right in the throat. Any harder she would have killed him. He flew back, clutching at his neck, falling to his knees and rolling onto his side. Moaning in agony.

"You'll be fine," she said.

He lie still on the deck, groaning. She took out his wallet. Inside she found a hotel card. Put it into her back pocket. Might be useful later. Then flipped through the rest of the wallet. Endless credit cards. Five different identities. The guy was an internet thief, for Christ's sake.

All of a sudden the world went upside down.

Lansing had a grip around her ankles. She was dangling over the side of the boat. All she saw was the blackness of the St. Lawrence River.

CHAPTER 7.2

Kiki had been hit so hard she didn't know what happened. Her body was flipped over. Her hands pained as they gripped the railing. All of her strength went into her upper arms. She hung on for dear life. The pain on her wrists was excruciating. She felt Lansing grabbing at her finger.

"You're going for a swim," he said to her.

But he couldn't get her hands loose from the railing.

"I'll show you." He walked away.

BAM!

He kicked her in the knuckles. Still, she kept a grip on the railing. Closed her eyes and concentrated deeply. She focused all her strength on her upper torso. On her core. Her body began to sway.

Up.

Down.

Up.

Down.

She gained momentum. Swung forward and lifted up over the railing to safety, facing the water.

Instinctively she kicked backwards.

AAAHH!

Lansing's screamed. Kiki turned around. She'd nailed him right in the shins. It seem like luck was on her side. As he clutched his lower leg she smacked him right in the throat. Pulled him towards her and hurled him over the railing.

But Lansing was too heavy. Kiki couldn't lift him in one go. His back was sprawled over the rail. He was trying to balance himself. She reached down and grabbed his ankles. Lifting him up—

BONK!

His head hit the side of the boat.

SPLASH!

Lansing was in the water. Oh no, she thought. What if he was unconscious? She was shocked. What if he drowns? Then another voice kicked in. He was going to kill you, you know.

She sat down. All she heard was the blare of orchestral music from speakers across the river. It sounded like Wagner. Nothing she recognized. Everyone was busy watching the light show. No one was paying attention to her. She looked around. No security cameras. No witnesses.

She reached over and grabbed Lansing's bag. Then sat down on a nearby bench. She looked at her hands. They were surprisingly okay. She hadn't even got a scratch. Hurt like hell, though.

She opened the bag and went through it. Inside she found a gun. And some printed out emails. This guy was living in the nineteenth century, wasn't he? She scanned the papers quickly.

Then she found a picture. Kiki was mildly

amused by the man's features. So this was the guy Lansing was supposed to meet. She searched the bag for any other sorts of credentials or anything else she might need to know. But there was precious little useful info. She got up and just happened to see Lansing's wallet. It had been flung onto the far side of the deck. She picked it up. It might come in handy.

She rejoined the crowds and watched the display. It was quite impressive. Bright abstract patterns flashed over the netting. The entire river was lit up with the brightness of lights. These were replaced by images of people's faces. Then a montage of old Quebec images. These dissolved into scenes from an old Hitchcock movie. Like it was from the fifties. No, not the fifties, the forties. 'I Confess.' With Cary Grant. She knew her Alfred Hitchcock. Her father and grandfather had made sure of that.

Her thoughts drifted to Angus. She had yet to get back to Scotland and put his affairs in order. For a moment she gazed into the blackness of the St. Lawrence River. Thinking about her grandfather. Sadness overwhelmed her. Over the last month her mind had been filled with thoughts of Ridley's pursuit and learning about nuclear weapons. There had been little time to think of much else. Now she felt like crying. She held back. Sat up. You've got to fake your way through a meeting with a hostile agent, she told herself. You've got to put on a show for this guy.

The ferry docked across the river at Levis. All the passengers poured out. She looked around. Followed the road to the train station. Crossed through a parking lot. To the poutine shack. Le Capitaine. She'd been there before. When she was a child. Her father and mother had taken her there on a vacation to Quebec City. It was getting late. Le Capitaine was getting ready to close. There were still people lined up for their fix of french fries, gravy, and cheese curds.

She looked around at the picnic tables. It didn't take long before she saw exactly who she needed to find. She sat down across from a man eating his dinner. A man wearing the clothes of a Catholic priest.

CHAPTER 7.3

"You know," the man said, "I don't believe in all this cloak and dagger."

"Is this your costume?" she said. "Your name is really Father Giancarlo?"

"My dear you must have faith. This is my Sunday best."

Great, Kiki thought. A fake priest with a lame sense of humor.

"I would like to know what you call this dish."

"It's called poutine."

"It's delicious. I wish we had this in Europe."

She couldn't place his accent. It could have been Italian. Of course it could also be Israeli or even Spanish. He had dark hair and features. From any Mediterranean or Middle Eastern country. At least she had a photo she could send back to the office.

"Now," he said, "I'm full. It's quite the meal, is it not?"

"It's good after beer. But if you eat too much of that you'll get fat."

"I suppose you would, my dear, wouldn't you? Well," he said, "shall we take the ferry back? I wanted to take in the light show."

"It's just killer," she said.

They boarded the ferry and slowly cruised back the way they came. It was smooth sailing all the way back to the Chateau Frontenac. As per the emails in Lansing's bag, she took him to room 1714. The key worked fine.

Giancarlo lay down on the bed. "So...now what?"

Now what? Kiki didn't have an answer. The e-mail didn't tell her what to do.

"Now... we..."

RING-RING!

They both froze.

RING-RING!

"Are you going to answer the phone?" asked Giancarlo.

Kiki reached over and picked up the receiver.

"Now, be very careful."

She almost threw up. It was Ridley's voice.

"What I want you to do," he said, "is go to the next room. In the drawer next to the Gideon's bible you'll find an envelope filled with your money. Leave the room key here, in the drawer in the nightstand. Take the one for room 1716. Half of your money will be in cash. The rest is in a money order. Stay there for five minutes. After that you may leave. We are watching the hotel. If we see you leave before that, you'll be putting your life on the line." The line clicked off. This was insane.

Her mind raced with thoughts of how she was being watched. They're going to find out who she was. She put down the receiver. "This is it for me," she said, picking up the key from the drawer. She departed without a parting glance to Giancarlo and went next door. The money was, as promised, next to the Bible. With a money order.

Her mind raced. How long before she was killed? But if they had seen her on the way in, they wouldn't be phoning the room. They'd have knocked at the door with a gun. And left her body in the bathtub. Or worse. No, she mused, this was amateur hour. Wasn't it? Just like her last adventure in Hamburg. The left hand didn't know what the right hand was doing. Her confidence was restored in the fallibility of criminals. They had over organized things to confuse the police. Lasing was probably a known criminal. Bait and switch. But Kiki wasn't a cop. They had no idea she was tailing them. Otherwise they would have cut the operation immediately.

They had to be completely incompetent. Or was it a trap? To convince her to join him? No, it couldn't be that, she thought. Ridley had enough brains to know she was loyal to her side of the game. She wasn't going to cross over. Not after she tried to shoot him. After he escaped in a helicopter in Hamburg.

There was only one thing to do.

KA-CLUNK!

The door to 1714 clicked shut. Father Giancarlo was off. She waited two minutes. What if someone was out there watching the hotel room? Aw, screw it. She'd go anyway.

She opened the door to the hall. Completely empty. Closed it behind her. Went to the stairwell. Opened that door. Looked around. Nobody. She scurried down as fast as she could. She was only on the third floor thank god.

She burst out of the stairwell on the ground floor. Took a side exit. Followed an adjacent alleyway until she made her way to the front courtyard taxi stand. Hiding behind some shrubs she watched Giovanni and another man get into a Cadillac Escalade.

Well, at least they chose a car that was easy to follow. As they drove off she got into the nearest taxi. The man was in the middle of eating a giant submarine sandwich.

"No," he said. "I don't think so. Take the other guy."

"Okay. But I was going to pay you a thousand bucks," she said in French. She pulled the wad of twenty-dollar bills out of her purse and waved it at him.

"What?" The guy perked up. "Okay, where do you want to go?"

"A Cadillac Escalade just pulled out of the parking lot. I want you to follow it. Right now. I'll pay you what ever is on the meter plus five hundred more for your troubles."

CHAPTER 7.4

It must've been after midnight when the Cadillac pulled off the highway at a rest stop. Kiki awoke as she felt the taxi making a hard right turn.

"What's going on?" she said.

"Ah, your friend. He's going to get a coffee, I guess."

"Can you do me a favor? Can you park somewhere secluded?"

"Why? You afraid that someone will see you?"

"Yes," she said.

"All right. You hungry?" he asked.

"Why?"

"Well you know, I was gonna get something to eat. And a coffee."

"You just ate. A footlong sandwich. Four hours ago."

"Yeah, but I'm a growing boy."

"Okay, sure. Get me a coffee—no—a hot chocolate."

"You want a doughnut?"

"No." Kiki couldn't understand the North American obsession with doughnuts.

Something she hadn't missed living in Europe. She took out her telephone. Snapped a picture of Father Giovanni from Lansing's files. She sent it to Tin Man. At this hour it was around five in the morning in Amsterdam. He probably won't be up for at least three or four hours minimum.

Her body struggled with the fatigue of jet lag. Normally she would never fall asleep in the back of a moving car.

The cab driver returned and they waited another twenty minutes for Father Giancarlo and the two other men to return to the Cadillac. They took off and continued down the highway. After five minutes they changed to a northbound route.

"It looks like they're going up to Val d'Or," the guy said.

"Where?"

"Northern Quebec."

"It looks like it's going to be farther than I thought."

"That's okay. I've gotten all kinds of crazy fares before."

"Really?" she said. "How long have you been doing this?"

"Oh, for the last fifteen years. I once had to drive Celine Dion to Toronto. It was the anniversary of Patsy Cline's death. She was feeling superstitious about airplanes. Decided she wanted to drive."

"That's nine hours on the highway."

"Sure. But she paid well. Then there were these three sailors I had to take to Halifax. They got drunk the night before. Missed their boat and it left without them."

"What? You drove all the way to the Atlantic Ocean?"

"Oh, yes. I've driven to New York as well. You'd be surprised the number of sailors that get stuck in Quebec City." He took a bite of a chocolate doughnut. "So, may I ask what you do?"

"I'm a secret agent," she said.

"Of course you are."

"I work with an international group of spies called Task Force Ten. We're based in Amsterdam."

"Don't you have a secret agent car? You know, a Ferrari or something? To drive?"

"I had to make plans at the last minute."

"Well you sure have a lot of money on you. You'd better be careful with all that. Do you have a bank account?"

"Don't worry. I'm not homeless."

"I am just asking, you know. A young girl like you. Comes into the back of my car with all that cash. Asks me to follow a car. I mean, it does seem a bit strange."

"I'll pay an extra two hundred if you keep your mouth shut."

"Sounds good to me," the driver said. "If you ever wanted to hide someone, north is where you'd want to go."

CHAPTER 8.1

They followed the Escalade for another five hours. It was getting closer to five in the morning when Kiki received a text message from Tin Man.

"Got picture. Will advise. We're sending package."

What the hell is that supposed to mean? Sending a package? How would they even know where she was? Kiki thought about it for a moment. Then realized they could probably track her cell phone.

The road narrowed to the point where it was shrouded by a canopy of evergreen trees.

For hours the windows had revealed nothing but dark bogs and forest. She was getting used to the idea that the road ahead wouldn't change much for the next hour or so.

Their target was a different matter. For most of the journey she'd been able to keep the Escalade in sight. But for ten minutes now she hadn't seen it.

"You've got to go faster. They might have turned off into the woods or something."

"Listen, they haven't turned off anywhere. We would've seen them," said the driver.

"And how do you know? You've got to speed up."

"I'm not speeding up. Do you understand? It's almost sunrise."

"And?"

"You know what happens when the sun comes up?"

"The birds come out?"

"And moose are going to come out, too."

"We're not going to hit a moose."

"You don't think so? I think you're one of those crazy girls." He took a sip from his travel mug. "You know, my brother, he's a cab driver in Montreal."

"Uh-huh."

"You know what happened to him?"

"I have no idea," said Kiki, impatient and tired.

"He had the exact same situation as you here tonight. These two girls flagged him down and offered him a big wad of cash. Like five hundred dollars. They had to go to a cabin in the Laurentians. But they wouldn't give him an exact address. You, know, the house number. He had no idea where they were going."

"And you're telling me this why?"

"They were trying to find the cabin that belonged to the new mayor of Montreal. All the guys before him had been arrested for corruption."

"That's tragic."

"And you know what was going on? He was up at this cabin waiting for these two girls."

Kiki decided she would play along. "Why was he waiting?"

"Turns out they were working. And they kept calling the mayor over and over again trying to get directions. And he kept trying to tell them where to go. And they couldn't find the place."

Kiki couldn't believe she had to sit through this. The cabbie had been so good. He hadn't talked for most of the trip. Now it was payback time.

"Do you know what he was wearing when he was talking to them?"

"No, I don't," said Kiki.

"Ladies' underwear. And a bra. He was paying these girls to come up to his cabin. They were gonna have a sleepover a party. Where they put on makeup and baked cookies. And then he'd have sex with them."

Kiki couldn't help but smile. "Well, you know, it can't be easy to find girls who will do that sort of thing."

"I'll tell you, these people. Some are so perverted. There was this one girl. I picked her up back in Quebec City. She said she was paid by a guy to watch him dress up in a tutu and do ballet. Afterwards she had to spank him and tell him he did a bad job."

"Are you going to catch up to the Cadillac?"

"Listen, the moose could be out any minute. If we smashed into a moose or a deer—"

A siren sounded.

Kiki saw the flashing red light behind them. Trouble. "You're going eighty, well below the speed limit, right?"

"Uh, maybe," said the cab driver

"Don't slowdown. Don't stop."

"I'm stopping for the police, you know."

"No. It might be someone impersonating a police officer. He can follow us if he wants to. Don't pull over. We have to stay behind the Cadillac."

"You're insane. I'm pulling over."

"No."

"Stop arguing." They pulled over.

Kiki watched through the rear window. It was some sort of motorcycle cop. Flashing only red lights. "Cops in Quebec don't have blue lights on their vehicles?"

"I don't know. Maybe it's different up here."

Fear gripped her. Anybody could attach a red light. One of Ridley's cohorts. Maybe somebody was tailing them. Making sure the Cadillac wasn't followed. We could be dead in a matter of minutes, she thought. Kiki looked back at the driver of the motorcycle. It wasn't a cop. She saw a helmet and a purple jumpsuit. On the side was a gun in a holster. This is not happening. She reached over and grabbed the door handle. Bolted out of the cab.

She ran into the woods. Immediately she descended into a thicket, grinding her escape to a halt. The sun was rising. But there still wasn't light enough that she could just run through the woods. It would be straight into darkness. She turned around and crouched down. Maybe she could stay hidden for a while. Long enough to figure out a plan.

She expected to hear a gunshot any second now. Whoever was on the bike would certainly kill the cab driver. She watched him get out of the vehicle. Chat with the person in the helmet. The two gazed out at the woods. Right in her direction. The cabbie just shook his head. The driver of the motorcycle took their helmet off. She couldn't quite make out the face.

"Kiki?"

"Huh?"

"Kiki, can you come out of the woods please?"

It was Jenny.

Kiki stood up. "What the hell are you doing here? How did you find me?"

"You have a cell phone, don't you? This little stunt you're pulling—this is not going over well back at the office. Dr. Digby will be very angry."

"Doctor Digby?" she said.

Jenny turned to the cab driver. "She gets delusions. But it's not a very severe form of schizophrenia."

"And she thinks she's a secret agent," the driver agreed.

"Kiki, pay the man his money. He's going to have to get a hotel room. Pay him at least a thousand dollars." Jenny turned to the driver. "Don't worry. I'll take care of this. Fortunately she's from a very wealthy family."

Kiki handed over the money to the man.

"You girls be careful. There's a lot of moose in these woods."

He got into the cab. Turned around and headed back towards Montreal.

"What the hell are you doing?"

"I'm following up a lead."

"Do you have any idea the shit you've caused?"

"Well, can I explain myself before you start hurtling accusations at me? What do you want to do? Are we going to a hotel?"

"No, we found a place. Turns out there's a safe house near here."

"A safe house? How much real estate do these people back in Amsterdam have?"

CHAPTER 8.2

The motorcycle roared down the Northern Quebec side roads at high speed. They'd already made two turns. Kiki had completely lost her sense of direction. Sun was streaming through the trees when Jenny slowed down and turned off at a small driveway. They got off the bike. Opened a gate that was padlocked. Jenny had the key. A dirt road lined with birch trees led to a clearing. And a small one-story log cabin.

Kiki looked around as she waited for Jenny, who unhooked two backpacks from the bike. "Pretty rustic, isn't it?"

"It's like we're on Walden Pond. You've got keys to this place?"

"Of course."

Inside was one big open room. There was a bathroom off to the side. Bunk beds occupied a corner. A fireplace at the back wall. The room was minimally furnished. It was unlikely any of the decor was younger than the late '70s.

Kiki walked into the kitchen area. Puke-colored faux-marble counter tops. She turned on the water. A sound like metal being pounded by a sledgehammer erupted from the bowels of the sink. Then brown sludge ran out of the faucet.

Jenny grimaced. "I'll go to town and get some bottled water."

"What is this place?"

"Thirty years ago it was a listing post for NORAD." Jenny flung open a circuit breaker panel and flipped some switches. A generator started up. Then she felt around the edges of the kitchen countertop. One edge had a hidden panel. It flipped down, revealing a console of switches, buttons, and knobs. She pressed a green button and flicked a switch.

Kiki felt the floor moving below her. She backed off as it rose up. Revealing a secret staircase to the basement. "What the hell is this?" she said.

Jenny flicked a couple of switches before she found the basement lights. The two of them walked downstairs. Jenny looked around. "Would you look at this..."

It was a rectangular room. Everything a sterile white—the walls, the floor tiles, the asbestos ceiling panels. Filled with early 80's-era communication equipment. All of it running, humming and beeping. Jenny shook her head. "Must have been a NATO outpost. In case of nuclear war. If the Ruskies got everybody else. Someone would still be able to broadcast instructions. I bet there's a radio tower somewhere out there in those woods."

Kiki poked at a dust-covered control panel. "Is there anything useful here?"

"Nah. I have no idea how to operate any of this."

They went back upstairs and closed the door.

"There's not much point in me being here," said Kiki.

"You might have been killed by now, you know."

"That, or maybe I would have pulled over to

the side of the road. And snuck into their—"

"You don't know where they were going." She opened her backpack and pulled out some maps. "But I do."

"Are we going hiking?"

"That road you were on? It's the long way to northern Ontario. But there are a couple of sites around here we can check out. Three or four abandoned mines. She looked up at Kiki. But you need to know there are people in Amsterdam who are really angry."

"I'm just trying to help."

"Going out on your own is really dangerous. This isn't a Hollywood movie where you rebel against the boss. Our job is to gather information. We're not cowboys."

"Is this an official lecture?" Kiki turned around and started unpacking her bag.

"I'm serious. Very few people are allowed to operate across national borders legally. If they arrest us, we have to be turned over to the Dutch government. But those agreements are very precarious—"

"Lots of people spy across national borders."

"Yeah, and they get kicked out all the time. We have special privileges. You know why? Because we don't shoot people. We gather information."

"Cut the BS. You and I both know you were hired because you're a Russian translator. Who also speaks German and Spanish. The rest of the girls were hired for the same reason. Including myself, I guess."

Jenny sipped from a bottle of spring water. "I have combat skills."

"Whatever. Point is, you people were hired as translators. That's what Mei told me. What do you know about operating in the field?"

"Look," said Jenny, "I know a hell of a lot more than you do. Because I've worked here for longer than a month." She took out a small box. Kiki immediately recognized it. A Geiger counter. "I know enough that I don't do surveillance in a cab." She finished the last of the spring water. "I saved you're ass back there. Do you know how long my journey has been? All to give you an alias? Miracles of miracles, maybe that cab driver is going to go back home and buy our cover story. Do you know how difficult that would normally be?"

"He wouldn't talk."

"Sure he would."

"You could have paid him off."

"That's not a magic bullet every time you screw up. You can't just bribe people. And I'm an American saying that. Do you know how much worse Digby's life is going to be for the next few days?"

"All I know is we got nothing done in the last month. Since I nearly died in an exploding building. Okay? I was the last person out. Taking risks while you left the scene of the crime."

"I follow orders. Because I want to stay alive. Beyond the tenure of my employment with Task Force Ten. NATO may get my allegiance, but it's not taking my life."

"If I hadn't gotten nosy we'd be back in Amsterdam. Scrolling through endless hours of airport security footage."

"Fine. Is that your only argument for flying halfway across the planet? On your own accord?"

"It's my ex-boyfriend behind all of this. I understand how he thinks. You don't. So cut me some slack before you get all presumptuous. Someone is out there in these woods. These people have taken ridiculous precautions. We're not going to stop them by checking a bunch of license plates and calling it a night."

CHAPTER 8.3

"Now this is important," said Jenny. "The area has three or four different mines."

It was the next day. They had taken time

to get proper rest. Recuperating from jet lag. Plotting. Talking. Getting updates on the local area from Tin Man and Digby. They were doing what Jenny wanted. Formulating a plan. They had just finished breakfast and were looking at a map of the local area.

"Now, of these four sites, two of them are active. Not a good place if you're going to hide something. But the other two, here—" she pointed at a nearby lake— "and here—" a second spot, adjacent to their cabin. "Strong possibilities. Both are abandoned copper mines. Yesterday the police sergeant took a look at this one—the site near us. I want to check it out first."

"And you think his report is reliable?"

"He seemed pretty certain of where the 'model airplane' landed." Jenny turned the map to Kiki. "The path is about two kilometers through the woods."

"What if we don't find anything?"

"I've arranged for natural resources to take us for an aerial tour of the area."

"Really? I'm going to get to ride in a helicopter?"

"It wasn't easy. So don't act like a tourist on a joyride." Jenny opened a kitchen drawer and pulled out a pistol and magazine.

"Do I get one?"

Jenny smirked. "After what I've seen you do in target practice? I don't think so. Do you have that cell phone of yours?"

"Of course."

"You know how to use it?"

"It's not difficult to use a telephone."

"I'm not asking if you know how to order pizza. It's the additional features I'm concerned about."

"Tin Man gave me a full briefing before I left for Barcelona. You don't need to worry."

"Good. And keep your eyes sharp."

"What if they spot us in the woods?"

Jenny's eyes narrowed. "You mean you didn't bring your moose costume?"

CHAPTER 8.4

"Be careful with that. Very careful." Giancarlo had instructed the two Belarusians to carry the cylinder of fissile material. And place it as close as possible to a workbench next to the drone.

"You must understand that this has only an eighty-five per cent chance of going right."

"And if it goes wrong?" said The Zebra.

"Everything within a thirty minute drive of this location could be destroyed."

"Should we ship it back to our American friends?"

"No, just don't blame me if this is the last conversation we ever have. Now, don't make any sudden moves." Giancarlo had brought a second device. A large case that carried a miniature robotic arm. Its base had a flip-out panel with a joystick control. He pressed a couple of buttons and two long narrow pieces of metal emerged. Both had pincers at the end of gyroscopic heads. He brought them up to the top of the main body of the aircraft. Slowly the pincers unbolted several panels on the top of the drone. The arms carefully removed the panels from the aircraft and placed them on an area marked off with bright yellow tape.

It took another hour and a half of work on the drone to make way for the weapon. The robot had each step of the process programmed. It performed without any human involvement. The men watched, interested at first, then just bored.

Giancarlo had designed the device with a German manufacturing firm about five years before. A company with experience building high-end aircraft. Allowing engineers to work in places that were difficult and dangerous for human beings. Few in the American government actually knew how many contracts were being tendered out to French and German aerospace firms. But there were a lot.

After the robot opened the nuclear 'cradle' as Giancarlo called it, he brought out the canister that contained the fissile material. "Now, this is the dangerous part. I'll have to do this manually."

He approached a small bank of computer screens. On a console set up behind a special wall of heavy lead. The other men joined him. He flicked a switch and was greeted by a small panel of knobs and buttons. With two mechanical handles to manipulate the robotic arms. A larger, more controllable version of the panel on the robot's case.

Above the controls were three small screens. One was a video feed. The other an infrared false-color image of the first screen. The third was some kind of spectrometer. The Zebra had no idea how to interpret it. He gestured to the monitors. "How will you know when things are going wrong?"

"You see this third screen over here?" He pointed to the spectrograph. "If that one goes haywire we're all screwed. Now, please be silent while I do this."

He manually manipulated the robotic arms with the handles. They unscrewed the top of the container with the nuclear weapon. Inside was a second heavy metallic lid. It revealed a small chamber. With a single golf ball-sized object. The top was round, with a small hook for the robot to grab hold. The base of the golf ball was cylindrical with a flat bottom. The robotic arm attached itself. Giancarlo pushed up on the left leaver ever so slightly. Slowly the nuclear device emerged from the canister. It went up through the air, towards the drone. It swung in a slow, deliberate arc towards the aircraft.

A bead of sweat dripped down Giancarlo's brow.

The Zebra and the Belarusians were silent with fear and awe.

Something beeped. The robot arm froze.

The Zebra's eyes widened. "What's going on?"

"Shhh," admonished Giancarlo.

He pressed a button. The beeping stopped. The arm continued on its journey.

"Only once we've got the aircraft's electronics back on... will we be completely safe. Please be patient."

The arm raised itself directly over the slot. Giancarlo made several minor adjustments so that its position exactly matched the nuclear cradle. One of the screens changed to a three-dimensional wireframe display. Giancarlo put on a pair of goggles.

He made a few more fine adjustments. When he was satisfied that the device was exactly where he wanted it, he slowly lowered the robot arm. Keeping his eye on the monitor. A pinging sound started. Like a sonar. The device got closer to the cradle. The pings became more frequent.

Lower and lower went the metal arm.

The pings came rapidly.

Giancarlo clenched his teeth.

The pings became a solid whine.

His hands clenched at the controls.

Silence.

Giancarlo let go.

Exhaled.

The Zebra saw his relief. "So it's done?"

"Be quiet. We have to be very careful." Methodically he sealed the cradle, panel by panel. After a few minutes he brought his laptop over and ran a program. "Just making a few checks," he said. When he got the results he wanted, he leaned over and flipped a bank of switches.

Giancarlo grabbed a nearby chair and sat down. "Looks like everything is okay."

"What was all the beeping?" asked The Zebra

"The beeping? Oh, it almost exploded." He took a swig of water. "Now, shall we go for breakfast?"

CHAPTER 8.5

"So that's where we're headed?" Kiki was looking through a pair of binoculars Jenny brought with her.

"That's it."

"I don't see anybody." Kiki took a last glance at the mine and lowered the binoculars. Handed them back.

Jenny stood up. "Yeah, well, you can never be too careful."

"Why don't we just walk over there? Go inside. There aren't any cars around."

"I'd just like to take a three-sixty before we head in. We're breaking and entering, you know."

"You're such a square."

"Well, when you're half-white, you don't get stopped by the cops that much, do you?"

Kiki rolled her eyes. They made a one-eighty degree pass around the warehouse through the woods. Sure enough, by the front garage door they spotted two men. They'd set up lawn chairs and a folding table to play cards.

"See," said Jenny. "I do know a couple things about what I'm doing."

"They're outside. They never would have heard us."

"Oh yeah? And what if you kicked down the door?"

"Do you have a skeleton key?" asked Kiki. She had learned the previous week that all members of Task Force Ten were issued a universal skeleton key. Guaranteed to open ninety-nine per cent of the world's locks. It had a special kind of electrified aluminum that allowed the key to mold itself into locks of a completely different shape. Kiki had left hers back at the cabin.

"Got it," said Jenny. "Someone could be inside. You've got those earbud microphones, right?"

Kiki nodded.

They found a door around the back of the hangar. The problem was that from the edge of the woods to the warehouse was at least two hundred meters of open ground. "We're basically sitting ducks," said Jenny. "There's nothing at all to hide behind."

Kiki looked around. "See anybody else?"

"Nope."

"What are we going to do?"

"Let's run for it."

They took off. Sprinting across the gravel pit towards the warehouse. They reached the door. Jenny signaled to Kiki, who put on her headphones. Listened carefully for a couple of minutes and then signaled. Inside—nobody. Outside—two guys.

From her pocket Jenny produced a set of keys. She unlocked the door. Silently they moved in.

Once inside Kiki's jaw dropped when she saw the drone. "What is that?" she whispered to Jenny.

"That's your model airplane."

The two of them walked around the side of the aircraft. Taking it all in.

Kiki's phone began buzzing.

"What is it?" said Jenny

Kiki took it out of her pocket. "It's a message from the Geiger counter in my backpack. The radioactivity in this room is extremely high."

"You mean this is nuclear?"

"Yeah. If we stay here for ten minutes we'll get half a year's dosage of radiation." She adjusted the controls. After a couple of seconds a map appeared on the phone. Showing the radioactive hot spots in the room. "I'm not a scientist, but it looks like it's coming from the center of the airplane." Kiki approached a canister on a nearby table. "And I'll bet this is where it came from."

Jenny smiled. "Illuminating. Is there anything that telephone can't do?"

"It can't order pizza."

"There must be a control device for the aircraft somewhere." They looked around the room.

Screaming erupted outside. In a Slavic language. Kiki and Jenny ducked down behind some fuel drums. One of the Belarusians opened the door. He was in a fierce argument with his gambling partner. He walked over to a picnic cooler. Grabbed a couple bottles of Coca-Cola. Then went back outside. Slamming the door shut.

"What was that all about?" asked Kiki.

"I'm not a perfect linguist," said Jenny, "but I'm pretty sure they were arguing over the poker game. One guy was not happy to lose."

"How do you know that?"

"I speak Russian. Pretty sure those guys are speaking Belarusian. Or Ukrainian."

Jenny took a closer look around the extremity of the room. "Kiki, over here."

It was a smooth black case. Large enough to hide a body. "What you think this is?"

"Open it and find out."

Kiki undid the locks. The inside was foam padded. There was a laptop computer and four grey boxes. "What do you think these are?"

"They look like hard drives."

Kiki placed her phone on one of the grey boxes. Automatically it launched an application. A graphic of a tower appeared. Scanning. Then a scroll bar. A few seconds later she heard the hard drive humming. After about a minute the scroll bar said one hundred per cent.

"Shouldn't you get them all?"

"There's four of them." An awkward pause from Jenny. "All right." Kiki got through the second one when Jenny motioned to her.

"Something's coming. A car. We've got to go."

"I'm almost done—"

"Close it down. Quick."

Kiki put away her phone and shut the case. As discreetly as possible. The two of them snuck out the back door. Kiki put on her headphones. She motioned for Jenny to be quiet. She waved her arm—run for it. Every bit of her body flooded with adrenaline as she sprinted across the black dirt.

They made it to the woods. Jenny checked

behind. No one had seen them. They kept running.

Back at the hangar, The Zebra walked inside. "It isn't much. I hope you guys like bacon and eggs," he said as he got a drink from the picnic cooler. He noticed a sliver of light. From the back of the hangar. He walked over. The back door was ajar. Ever so slightly.

Something was wrong.

CHAPTER 9.1

"Stop," Jenny said to Kiki. "Find a cover position. Nine o'clock."

"Huh?"

"To the right. Get down and be quiet. If one of us gets hurt, the other runs for safety. Clear?"

"Yeah."

"Keep at a right angle. Don't bunch together. Better to give them two things to shoot at than just one."

For five minutes they sat, obscured by bushes and trees. Until Jenny was satisfied no one was following them. "I think we're in the clear. If they were pursuing, they'd be here by now."

They continued back towards the cabin. "What you think was going on back there?" asked Kiki

"You saw the markings on that plane. It's American."

"Are you saying the U.S. military is in cahoots with my ex-boyfriend?"

"I wouldn't put it past them, given how corrupt some of these people are. But it's a little hard to imagine anybody in the United States government would let a nuclear bomb fall into the hands of these clowns."

Kiki snapped a twig. She wore a pair of knee high riding boots from Alexander Wang. They were meant for plane travel. Not exactly the best choice for the terrain. At least the heels on them weren't too bad. "What if someone went nuts and just stole it? Look what happened to Straub in Hamburg. He was working with the German government, wasn't he?"

Jenny shook her head. "It just doesn't smell right. Look at where we are. Why would they land a drone here? Unless you're planning a sneak attack? The aircraft can go anywhere. There are far better places for the air force to hide it." She pushed a tree branch out of her way. "Upload the data to Tin Man. He'll figure out what to do with it."

"I only got half of what was on those hard drives. It won't be much use."

"If these people were smart enough to steal something like this—assuming the drone is stolen—who knows what else they've got planned."

"Wait a minute." Kiki stopped. "This is our typical mentality. It's easy to think that these criminal elements are smarter and more devious than we are. But my grandfather never believed that. If it were true they could probably make more money working in the private sector."

"Yeah, I guess. As long as they're not fanatics. Or out for revenge."

Kiki shook her head. "Ridley is very good looking. But he's not the sharpest knife in the drawer. I'm willing to bet he hasn't thought through his exit strategy at all."

"You honestly believe that?"

"They may have a plan. I bet it's a good one. As long as it goes right. But if something goes wrong they might not know what to do. A successful terrorist attack happens," said Kiki, "because no one tries to stop them. We're already on their case."

"That's a good point," said Jenny. "But we're making a big assumption."

"What's that?"

"That they're not following us. You leave a trail of bread crumbs pretty much everywhere you go."

CHAPTER 9.2

"Look at this." Ridley was crouched down, examining the gravel pit behind the warehouse.

"I don't see it," said Giancarlo.

"Somebody has walked through here. And recently."

"You're being paranoid. Fantasizing about every which way things could run amok."

"I'm telling you," said The Zebra, taking a second look at the ground. "There's no way I left that door open."

"How do you know?" said Giancarlo. "I saw you go through it not five minutes before we left for town."

The Zebra shook his head. "I'm telling you something is wrong here."

"The equipment is working fine. You want to spend the next two days running after ghosts in the woods?" said Giancarlo

The Zebra nodded. "I'm not going to do it. You are."

"Why me?"

"Because your job is done for now. Ridley stays here. I'm the one making sure everything goes well for Katarina. You're not busy. Take a little trek through the woods. It won't hurt you. Besides," he said, patting Giancarlo's stomach, "you could use the exercise."

"And what if I find someone?"

"Take one of the guards with you. He's got a gun."

"I want a weapon, too."

"There might be a pocket knife around somewhere," said Ridley.

Giancarlo was not amused. "What if it was the police?"

"They've already been here, and found nothing," said The Zebra. "If they were to arrive, it would be in force. It's probably a hunter. Or one of the local kids. Or just a curious onlooker."

"Is it possible someone knows we're here?"

"Unlikely. That's why Lansing was careful. And a great distraction. The genius of using him as a go-between. No one is going to wonder about who he talks to, but they'll probably want to interrogate him," said The Zebra. "And he'll give them all the wrong answers."

"Yeah," said Ridley, "he's a magnet for the police."

Giancarlo was puzzled. "Who are you talking about?"

"The man who escorted you to the hotel. You know, the American."

"What American?"

"From the ferry. The person who brought you across the river."

"I have no idea who you're talking about." Giancarlo showed signs of nervousness.

"You came by ferry?"

"Yes."

"And a man escorted you to a hotel room?"

"No."

"What do you mean?"

"It was a petite twenty-two year old girl." Giancarlo went on to describe her in detail.

Ridley was aghast. "It can't be—"

"It probably is," said The Zebra. "Something's wrong here. We've got to move. This could be real trouble."

CHAPTER 9.3

"What you mean it's not working?"

"I don't know. We've only got some of the data. It's just a pile of meaningless code," said Jenny.

Kiki was getting upset. "I don't understand. Even so, it should be usable."

"Look at it. Look at the screen."

Kiki glanced over. It was indeed a pile of random data that made no sense.

"It only opens as a text file."

"Can we upload it to Tim Man?

"I don't know. It won't copy from your phone."

"What do you mean?"

"It's like it's been encoded not to leave wherever it is. You scanned and copied it. But it won't transfer over the Internet or any of the cables. It won't let itself be duplicated."

"There must be a way to get it off the phone."

Five minutes later Tin Man was on the line from Amsterdam.

"Look, you know, I don't understand why it would do that. It must be some sort of security protocol. Recognizes the data has been moved to another system. It's preventing it from accessing the computer's base memory. A kind of digital dongle."

"A what?"

"A dongle. Like a key," said Tin Man. "Except this data knows you're trying to use it on the wrong computer, so it won't move. It's like trying to take a book out of the library. With a security sensor. That hasn't been deactivated. It sets off an alarm and the guard comes to stop you. Well, this is the coding equivalent of that. You see, your phone sends a light electric charge through the hard drive. Creates a molecular cascade that causes the coding on the drive to activate for one-thousandth of a second so that—"

"You lost me at electric charge."

"It basically does a digital smash and grab. Everything in sight. It's kind of like a herd of elephants stampeding across the Sahara. It's gonna kick up a storm. Take the wind with it, you know."

"Okay," said Kiki, "but what do you want me to do?"

"I'll have to fly over there and take a look at it myself. If the drone is still on the ground, we don't want it to get out of our sight."

"That makes no sense at all," said Jenny. "We should try to get some info first. Find out why this drone is here. Maybe we should just call the police."

"No, they don't want local authorities involved. That would get it in front of the media. It might be a secret operation on behalf of the military."

Jenny shook her head. "We didn't see any soldiers. And wouldn't they land it at the military base, instead?"

"Look," said Tin Man, "I don't really want to go to America, but the word has already come down from on high. We're making plans on how to logistically movie the office to where you are."

"Why can't we just go back to Europe?"

"That cabin you're in has a radar unit capable of tracking all flights in the area. You guys will get to learn how to operate it until I get there. That way we'll all be in the same place. No one wants that drone out of our sight. No one, outside of Task Force Ten and the committee, even knows it's there."

Kiki caught something out of the corner of her eye. "We've got to go." She motioned to Jenny. "Look, in the yard."

She saw a figure approaching from the woods.

Jenny motioned to her to get down and got out a gun.

Kiki moved to the wall and crouched down underneath the window. Jenny snuck across the floor and took a quick peek outside before ducking down. Then took out a pair of headphones from her pocket and found a small stick. She wrapped one earbud around it. Inside the earbud was a micro camera. Displaying a video stream on the telephone. She pushed the microphone jack earbud up towards the windowsill. Two men were in the yard.

Jenny signaled two fingers to Kiki. Giancarlo, still dressed as a clergyman, got closer. He looked right through the window. Jenny put the stick with the camera down.

Kiki glanced over to the kitchen and saw a reflection in a toaster.

As Giancarlo moved back away from the window, Kiki and Jenny scurried around to hide out of sight. Jenny used her earbud camera to get a clear view of the room while they crouched behind the kitchen counter. She saw Giancarlo look through the kitchen window. He tried the door.

There were a couple of bangs. Then he kicked the door open.

"What is all this? It looks like somebody's drinking shed. There's nothing here. No one's been around for months. Let's go."

The door slammed shut. Kiki and Jenny looked at each other with relief. Kiki pointed to the window. Jenny aimed her camera back over the windowsill. On the phone's screen they saw Giancarlo and the Belarusian guard disappear into the woods.

"Okay, we're safe. But we've got to get out of here."

"How did they not see any of our stuff?"

"Well, they're obviously stupid. There are hard drives on the floor behind the couch. They just took a glance and left." Jenny grabbed her laptop from a hiding spot and placed it on the coffee table. Flipped it open and redialed the Amsterdam office.

"Listen," said Tin Man, after they re-established the connection. "I've figured it out. I need a couple minutes of you time."

"We don't have a couple minutes."

"I'm telling you you've got to give it five min—"

"You'll figure it out. We have to find a new location. This one has been compromised."

"No. You cannot leave that site. There's something in the basement that will help. A code machine."

"We can't," said Jenny

"Listen," said Kiki, "we almost just got shot. This is not happening right now."

"Fine," said Tin Man, "if you insist."

They left and gathered the equipment as quickly as they could. In the yard they surveyed the edge of the woods to make sure no one was there. "I think we're okay," said Kiki.

They packed the bike. Got on the back. Jenny tried to start it.

"Something's wrong. I left my keys here just a few minutes ago."

"What do you mean?" said Kiki. "What are we going to do, call a cab?"

"Maybe that's exactly what you'll have to do," said a man's voice.

It was Giancarlo. He removed Kiki's helmet. Next to her was the Belarusian, pointing a shotgun right at her head.

CHAPTER 9.4

"You don't think Ridley would simply let you go about your business without any sort of monitoring, do you? We're his insurance plan."

"Oh really?" said Giancarlo. "I don't think that's true at all. I think you're a liar. And I think this is all a ruse."

They were back at the cabin. Giancarlo was looking through the contents of Jenny's backpack. "Doesn't look like too much stuff. I don't see any evidence you're here to go camping for the weekend. Where's your marsh-mallows and hot dogs? And that American thing you love the most, hamburgers."

"We didn't get our grocery shopping done yet," said Jenny.

"I loathe hamburgers." Giancarlo motioned

to the Belarusian guard, who put down his shotgun. Instead he picked up a piece of rope that was lying on the couch. "Tie her up, but the black girl is staying with me. She has some interesting things to say, doesn't she? What's your name?"

"My name is Foxy Brown."

"You're funny. You think I don't get your American jokes." He turned to the guard. "Tie up her friend. We're going to kill her if she doesn't tell us what's on the computer."

Jenny leaned forward. "Why don't you have a look for yourself?"

Giancarlo took out the laptop. He hit the 'on' button. As soon as his finger made contact, he screamed, an electric shock running up his arm. The smell of smoke and burnt flesh drifted up from the keyboard. He shook for a moment and collapsed to the floor. The guard just looked at him, unsure of what to do. After a moment Giancarlo pushed himself up. Clenched and released his fists. His muscles ached. But his energy was still there. He got to his feet.

"What is this?" he cried as he ran over and slapped Jenny in the face. "What have you done to me?"

"I guess it doesn't like you," she said.

Giancarlo bent down, nursing the bruise on the side of Jenny's cheek.

"You hit like a sissy," she said. Jenny glanced at the blackened, charred skin on his fingers. "Don't worry. It'll heal in a few hours. It's not serious. It's there to discourage thieves. People who might get nosy. It won't actually hurt you. Or leave a scar."

"Interesting. Now, I want you to unlock the computer," he said. "Or we'll take the shot gun and kill your friend."

The guard pushed the shotgun's barrel to Kiki's head. "The code or she dies."

Jenny didn't flinch. Giancarlo realized she couldn't see Kiki from the angle of the chair. "That gun—it's pressed to the head of a human being. His finger might twitch. Any minute now."

Thoughts raced through Jenny's head. She made a mental inventory of the hard drive's contents. Nothing on it was worth Kiki's life. "Okay," she said. "Fine." Jenny unlocked the computer.

Giancarlo examined the interface. Clicked through menus and programs. "Looks like you've taken all the games off it." He opened a folder buried under several others.

"What is this? The coding you have here? On the drive?" He scrolled through the lines of data. Giancarlo recognized what it was. "This won't do. You've got something that belongs to me."

"This is important?"

"Oh, it's very important. Now lets see. We'll

deal with your friend in a moment. You," he said to the security guard, "leave the white girl. I'll deal with her alone." He pointed to Jenny. "Take her outside and kill her."

"What?" Panic filled Jenny's face.

The guard led her outside by the front door. Giancarlo turned to Kiki.

"Now, you're going to answer some of my questions. What were you doing meeting me in Quebec City?"

"Just lucky I guess."

"I'm serious."

"Why don't you take me back to Ridley? We'll talk it all out. Together."

"No. Out of the question. I think you and him have the same information. You're involved together in this somehow. If I don't get rid of you soon, there'll be trouble. Even if you're not working with each other, I think he might have a soft spot for you." Giancarlo leaned it to her face. Intimately close. "What's your name? Kiki? Is it?"

"No," Kiki said, staying on the word just a bit too long.

Giancarlo moved back, stood up straight. "You're lying. I can tell." He looked to the window, contemplating. "I know what we're going to do. I'm going to take a knife. I want to see how far I can get cutting your arm before you tell the truth. Don't worry. I'll stop whenever you feel like it. But if you tell me what you know, I'll let your friend out there live."

"How do I know you won't kill me no matter what I say?" she said.

"You don't. But the man out there is going to kill her in less than three minutes. If you tell me everything that's going on, we won't hurt you. We'll let you run away. Right now."

"What if we got the police?"

"Doesn't matter. We'll be long gone before they show up. Don't you think we thought about that?"

While this conversation was going on, Kiki had managed to untie the knot the Belarusian had sloppily tied around her wrist. It was one of the few skills that Angus, her grandfather, had taught her. Along with karate, she knew how to get out of nearly any knot in the world. Silently. Especially when trapped in a chair. In fact, this was the exact situation that Angus had prepared her for. She had already managed to get it half off. All she had to do now is keep him talking a little longer.

"I'll tell you everything you need to know. I just don't want you to hurt Jenny."

"Jenny, that's her name is it?"

"Yes," said Kiki. "We work for—how should

I put it—we work for an organization. We're freelancers."

"Oh yeah, that's interesting. And why did you come here?"

"Everybody knows what's going on. What you're doing."

"Really? I don't think anyone has any idea."

"Oh yes, they do. Everyone knows exactly your plan. By the time this conversation ends there will be no less than three different intelligence organizations after you."

"Really? So where's Ridley headed after this? Tell me."

Kiki drew a blank. She had no idea. But the best thing she could do is sow the seeds of a conspiracy in Giancarlo's mind. It was what he wanted to hear. "He's going to..." Kiki's eyes darted around the room. "California."

"Wrong answer." Giancarlo picked up a curtain rod. Lying on the floor by the window. "All right. You didn't tell the truth. I'm going to have to punish you."

Behind her, Kiki had already escaped her bindings. As he moved closer she stood up, grabbed the chair, pulled it up in front of her. A barrier between them. Like a lion tamer. She pushed forward and drove him into the window.

"Ahhh!" Giancarlo was shocked. Winded by

the impact of one of the chair's legs. Right in the stomach. He gasped for air as he swatted at her with the curtain iron. With one big heave he pushed the chair back. As hard as he could.

She toppled over the sofa behind her. And onto the floor behind it.

BANG!

Outside there was a huge loud noise.

BANG!

A gunshot!

Giancarlo looked out the window. "Oh my god."

CHAPTER 10.1

Kiki's head was swimming. As she rolled over the couch, her head smacked off the floor. She saw Giancarlo rushing out the door. There was more shouting.

BOOM!

Another shotgun blast. There was yelling. Screaming.

SMASH!

Someone crashed through the window. Kiki crawled over. Tried to stand up. Still blacking in and out of consciousness. Kiki had to sit down.

There was another slam against the wall.

She heard the sound of a motorbike starting.

"Kiki!" It was Jenny. Outside. "Do something."

"Huh?" Kiki said, still dazed. She stood up and ran out the front door. In front of her Giancarlo had somehow managed to get Jenny's motorcycle started. He swung around the front yard. Sped out of the driveway.

Kiki whipped around and saw Jenny. "Are you okay?" she said.

"I'm fine."

"What happened to you?"

"I was in a fight with Giancarlo and a chair. The chair won."

"Did someone fire a gun?"

Jenny was silent.

Kiki looked around. She saw a pair of legs. On the grass behind the cabin. She moved in closer. Only then did she see the body of the Belarusian. Nausea overwhelmed her. The side of his head had been blown off. His abdomen was a mess.

She'd never been this close to a dead body. Bile rose up her esophagus. Uncontrollably. She vomited onto the grass.

Jenny consoled her. Rubbing her back.

"I'm sure it's just me being hit in the head."

"I'll take you to the hospital."

"No, no, I'll be okay."

"It's been a long time since I killed someone," said Jenny, gazing at the body.

"You killed someone before?"

"Yeah. It's not pleasant."

"Well, I think I might have killed someone earlier. On a boat," said Kiki. "It's not your fault, you know. He was going to hurt you."

"They were going to hurt both of us."

Kiki rubbed spit off her lips. "We're in an awful lot of trouble. How are we going to explain this?"

Jenny shot her an astonished look. "What do you mean, explain?"

"What do you expect to do? We just leave the drone there and hitchhike our way to the nearest motel?"

"No. We'll give headquarters a call. Then we're calling the police. They can deal with whoever's squatting at that old mine."

"And we are going to do what, after that?"

"Go inside and find a deck chair. We'll sit back and watch. Our part in this is over."

CHAPTER 10.2

Ridley was a hundred meters from the warehouse. Smoking. He heard the noise of a dirt bike. Who could that be? Somebody might be investigating.

He stubbed out the cigarette in the gravel and ran towards the Belarusian guard. "Here—get inside," he said. "And get me some binoculars."

He followed the guard inside and got behind a window. He took the binoculars and glanced outside. It was Giancarlo. Ridley walked out and greeted him with open arms. "What are you doing here? Where did you get that?" he said.

"We haven't got time. The operation has been blown."

"What do you mean?"

"Any minute now the police will be here. That girl you told me about? She's some sort of secret agent. Half a kilometer through those woods they've been surveilling us. For days. Maybe weeks."

"When you mean?" said Ridley.

"There was a black girl with them as well."

"Jenny," said Ridley. "I knew this would happen."

"What do you mean, you knew this would happen? You said you were secure."

Ridley wasn't happy. This was a disaster. All focus would be on him. He was sure to take the blame. They would demand to get rid of him. "Of course. I took every precaution."

"You brought them here, didn't you? These

were your old associates. This is all your fault."

The Zebra emerged from the hangar. "What's going on?"

"Him. This guy. Over here. He's brought these agents down on us. Now they'll probably get the police, too. Any minute now."

The Zebra remain calm. Dispassionate. He'd been preparing for this. "What happened to Sergei?"

Giancarlo looked at him, puzzled. He hadn't thought of the guards as real people, with names. "Your douchebag private security? He's dead. Shotgun shell to the brain. The negress from America saw to that. I stole their dirt bike. They have no other vehicle to get away. As far as I can tell."

The Zebra thought for a moment. "We need to get this aircraft up and out of here." He turned to Giancarlo. "Get with Griorgi over there. I need you to take a survey of our position and get the guns together."

"What? I have to get out of here. There's no way I'm sticking around."

"Your job is done."

"No, it's not. They've got information."

"What?"

"Yes. On the negress's computer. I've got to get that back. Otherwise the mission will be compromised." Giancarlo's blood pressure began to rise. "We could be locked up and flown to a Jordanian prison. All because you hired discount help."

The Zebra remained cool. "Don't get angry. It will impair your decision-making ability. We've got to get the aircraft launched. Do the starter procedures."

They rushed around opening the hangar doors. Inside, Ridley manned the drone's remote control panel. A deafening roar erupted as the engines started up.

The Zebra and the remaining guard opened the back of the Escalade. Found another crate. Brought it back to the warehouse. Inside the box was a cache of pistols and shotguns. And at least three hundred rounds of ammunition.

Giancarlo shook his head. "Well, we're in real trouble now, aren't we?"

The Zebra loaded a pistol. "You get the plane. Get the control panel out of here. I'll deal with the negress and the police. We'll try to give you time to escape. Provide some cover. We'll get out as we can. The front way. If possible."

"What if you die?" said Giancarlo.

"I'm not going to die. Not here. I've got a plan. Don't you worry."

Over at the controls, Ridley guided the drone out of the hangar. It rolled out onto the runway. A warning light went off on the panel. "Something's wrong. There's a fuel cap loose. Useless incompetent morons. They can even fill a plane without help."

Ridley and Giancarlo rushed to the left wind, only to see a trail of liquid spewing from the side of the aircraft.

Giancarlo took charge. "Here, help me. Grab that ladder."

Ridley got up on top of the plane. He took the wrench and unbolted the fuel connection pump.

"It's jammed."

Giancarlo shook his head. "Try harder."

Soon enough they got the pump off. Giancarlo tossed up a pair of pliers. He knew exactly what the problem was. Ridley attached the fuel gage. Then closed the hatch tightly.

"I don't know if that'll hold."

"We don't have any options, do we?"

Ridley raised his head. Off in the distance he heard sirens. "We've got to get this thing in the air."

"Fine."

They ran back to the control panel. "We're ready to go," Ridley told The Zebra, whose cool composure was betrayed by beads of sweat on his forehead.

Deep in the woods, on a dirt road, Kiki and Jenny were in the back seat of a patrol car. There had to be at least five vehicles heading towards the mine.

"And you're sure this is the place?" said the policeman. Sergeant Goudain. "You better be telling the truth."

"Listen, we weren't lying to you," said Jenny. "All this will be clear in a few hours. They'll probably have heavy armaments. You want to take this slow."

"Don't worry. Serge up there can handle anything," said the officer.

Jenny looked at him with an air of disbelief. She got the feeling the Sureté officer wasn't taking her seriously. "There will be nothing left of Serge if he's not careful."

Overhead came a sonic boom. At high speed the drone shot past, so low it filled the sky above the vehicles.

"How did they get it in the air so quickly?" asked Goudain.

Jenny shook her head. "I don't know. Maybe these things were built for speed."

Back at the warehouse Giancarlo and Ridley were packing up.

"You got everything? The panel and the beacon?"

Giancarlo was carefully loading the motorbike. "I don't know what we're going to do with all this gear."

Ridley grabbed some bungee cords. Wrapped them around the back part of the scooter. Just above the back wheel. "That'll do for now. Keep a hand on the box. Ride with one arm around me, the other hand on the cords. It's gonna be bumpy."

"Do you have the map?"

Ridley shook his head.

The Zebra approached. Showed them a topographical map. "I don't know everywhere this thing goes. Could be off a cliff. Be careful. This should get you back to Val D'Or. To the main highway. It's an old logging road that hasn't been used for twenty years."

"Don't worry," said Ridley. "We'll be fine. Let's go."

He jumped on the bike and Giancarlo followed. They took off at the highest possible speed. Disappeared into the forest.

The Zebra pointed to the sole remaining guard. He switched into Russian. "Take up position by the door. Cover the main entrance to the hangar. And the top of the road. Over here." He indicated towards the side of the Cadillac.

As the motorbike's engine dissipated the

sound of sirens got closer and closer. "The first one you see, you take out. Okay?"

The Sureté patrol SUV burst up the driveway.

Immediately the Belarusian fired his shotgun. Took the driver by surprise. The officer turned sideways in an attempt to avoid the spray of bullets. Only to make it worse, lining up the vehicle in the Zebra's sight.

The Zebra ran closer to the patrol car and hurled a grenade. It landed by the side and rolled under the gas tank at the back.

KABOOM!

The whole thing went up in flames. Including the two officers inside. They screamed in agony.

Three patrol cars back, Kiki and Jenny were shocked. "What is going on?"

"Get away. Get down." Goudain waved them back. The two got out and ran. Stopping at the edge of the road.

The rest of the police joined them at the edge of the woods. Goudain turned to Kiki and Jenny. "How many did you say?"

Kiki was confused. "I don't know. There can't be that many. Three. Five at most."

Six officers gathered behind a patrol truck.

"Fan out towards the woods," said Goudain. "Keep your positions wide. And broad. We'll take them from the far corner."

Kiki and Jenny moved off to the side. Kiki

looked up at Sergeant Goudain. "We're going to go into the woods."

"Yeah, you better—"

KABOOM!

Another patrol truck exploded.

"Get out of here."

They ran. Kiki was sure she would trip. But she didn't. The bullets didn't follow them, either.

At the warehouse The Zebra and the guard were focused mainly on a single patrol truck that had just exploded. They were laying down fire to keep the cops away. But they were aiming along the same line. Neither noticed the line of officers spreading off to their right.

Fifty or so meters from the entrance to the warehouse Jenny found a log that gave decent cover. She crouched down behind it. Kiki lay down next to her.

Jenny got out a small pair of binoculars.

Kiki leaned over to her. "What's going on?"

Jenny watched. "It looks like a man in the doorway. He just ran away from the SUV. Then someone else by the hangar door. Firing towards the police."

The cops fired back.

BOOM BOOM BOOM!

Three shots hit the man in the door. The Belarusian was knocked down.

Four officers scampered up to the wreckage of the lead patrol truck.

"Can I see?" said Kiki.

"I think they've got a grenade out. Or maybe it's a smoke bomb. I don't know." Jenny focused on a line of three officers getting in close. "It's a can of tear gas. They're going to toss it into the hangar. To smoke them out."

One brave officer ran up to the door where the guard had stood and tossed a tear gas bomb inside, then ran away.

BANG!

Inside, the tear gas exploded. Showering sparks onto the floor. The Zebra turned around. Some of the sparks hit the trail of gasoline left by the drone. The trail ignited. Racing towards the half-dozen fuel tanks in the back.

kaaaaa BBOOOOOmmmmm!!!!!

The entire warehouse exploded in a fireball.

Kiki looked at Jenny. "You think they're going to take us back to the station for this?"

CHAPTER 10.3

"Look," said Kiki, "this is just the way things are. It was unfortunate. But it was him or us. You know, you can speak to me in French. I understand French."

Kiki sat in the interrogation room at the back of the Senneterre sureté station. In front of her, the half-eaten remains of a McDonald's hamburger and french fries. That was as much food as she'd gotten for the last 4 hours. She was sitting in some sort of office chair. It was at least thirty years old. The lighting was harsh. The tables still had an ashtray in case she wanted to smoke. Mirrored glass at the far wall. And a video camera in the upper corner of the room.

"You can speak to me in English. I get more out of speaking in English," said Sergeant Goudain.

"We're not your enemies," said Kiki. "You've got to understand. We've been over this four or five times—"

"I think your friend said something different."

"No, she didn't."

"Yes, she did. She said you killed the man in the yard."

"Look, I get what's going on. Some terrible things happened. And people died. The media is on your case. You need to give them something. But I'm telling you this is important. You must say nothing about these people. Or this incident."

"Not even about a stolen military drone?"

"Nothing. Because once that gets out, these people—the bad guys—will be panicked. The people who are doing this, they have a plan and a schedule. If you let them know you're on to them, they might just move their timetable forward. Before we can catch up. They might just drop this thing on New York or Boston or Montreal. Minutes later."

"You are saying we shouldn't tell the US army? They'll be able to stop it."

"I don't have a lot of confidence in that. There also might be someone on the inside. They couldn't get this far on their own. And even if you stop the drone, you've got people who will probably try again."

"You think it has a nuclear bomb on it?"

Kiki realized what she was saying sounded ridiculous. "I'm just trying to paint a picture. Of possible outcomes."

"I don't know if I should believe you or not.

You come here. At first you don't talk. Then you defend your friend."

"Look, don't try to play me—"

"Your friend, she's already gone. She just left you behind."

"No, she hasn't. She's in the next room. This can go on as long as you want. My story is not going to change."

"You sure?"

"Look, we're going to need your help. Right? And they're going to ask me, how was Sergeant Goudain? Was he cooperative? If I say good things, everything will go smoother."

"You're not the one with two dead officers."

"I'm not having this conversation with you because I want a promotion. I want to bring their killers to justice. Three of them are dead. The other two are probably out of the country by now. This isn't some outlaw biker gang or people growing marijuana plants. Or some inbred hick with a grudge. We're talking about international terrorists. And they're not going to stop. Every moment I spend here will make it harder to put an end to all this. We're on the same side, you know."

There was a knock on the door. One of the officers, a young woman, came in. She whispered something into Sergeant Goudain's ears.

"What? I don't know," he said in French. "I don't think, you know."

The woman shook her head.

He turned back to Kiki. "Look, I need you to come back here."

"I promise."

"And you have to testify about what happened. There's going to be an inquiry—"

"Fine," said Kiki. "I have no problem. With any of that. But I need to do my job."

In the office Jenny was talking to a tall, handsome man. Kiki was impressed. He was dressed in a suit. Then she took a second look and recognized the face. "Who are you?"

"My name is Hawthorne Steele."

"We've met before," she said.

"Yes. I was around on a couple of different occasions. In different attire."

"You were in Quebec city—"

"Yeah, that was me."

"How did you know my housemate's name?"

"I know a lot of things about you."

Kiki's eyes narrowed. "What are you, like, the CIA?"

"No. I'm a freelance contractor. Though I usually work for the CIA. Today I'm helping out NATO and your friend Digby. Because no one wanted to make the long drive up here to get you out of jail."

After some formalities and a few more

questions—and the promise Kiki would return for a full inquiry in front of a judge and prosecutor—they were allowed to go.

In the parking lot Steele directed both of them towards his car.

Kiki was surprised. "Oh my god, you actually drive around in this?"

It was at least ten years old. A Ford Taurus.

"I said I'm freelance. Which means I have to pay for the car out of my own pocket. Although they subsidize a few things."

"What kind of things?"

"I'll tell you over poutine," he said.

CHAPTER 10.4

"To tell you the truth, this is the first time I've had to deal with girls. This business, at least on the operative side, tends to be more of a sausage party." Hawthorne took a sip of Molson Export. Water dripped off the bottom of the bottle. Which he tried to mop up with a small paper napkin. Ineffectively.

Kiki and Jenny sat across from Hawthorne in the dining lounge of the Auberge Grand-Montagne in Labelle, Quebec. They had been on the road for the past four hours. And had settled in for the night. The place was out of the way. A truck stop kind of motel. Innocuous. Completely surrounded by forest. Mostly noteworthy as overflow accommodations for Mount Tremblant, which was nearby.

At check-in, Hawthorne made a badly mangled attempt at French. Kiki had to step in and do the translating.

The woman at the counter was surprised they had any vacancies. "Usually the whole thing is full in the summer," she said. The woman hesitated before handing over the keys.

"What is it?"

"One thing," she said. "Make sure you keep the glass doors to the patio closed."

"Why?" said Kiki.

"The bears. They might try to, you know, mosey into your room. Especially if you have any food out. Or beer." Jenny and Hawthorne were amused by this.

After a brief check for bedbugs, Kiki met them in the lobby. As she arrived she noticed Jenny and Hawthorne were getting along quite well.

"Sorry to keep you guys waiting."

They were having a discussion about, of all places, Baltimore. "Actually we're both from the suburbs," said Jenny. "Anybody from

Baltimore knows it's a pretty rough place. His dad worked in Maryland, near Washington. My father worked in the same sort of area."

"What? For the CIA?"

"No," said Hawthorne. "The CIA campus is in Virginia. That's south of Washington."

After that they had gone into the restaurant where Kiki introduced Hawthorne to poutine for the first time.

"This is amazing," he said. "I can't believe there's cheese in the french fries."

"Don't you have Coney Island fries in the States?" she said.

"That's only in New York."

The restaurant's menu was hard to get excited about. There was fresh caught trout. But everything else was mostly hamburgers and steak. Kiki settled on a Caesar salad.

"The thing you have to understand," said Hawthorne, "is what we used to do thirty or forty years ago with security intelligence has been farmed out. You guys—I don't understand how you got government jobs."

"Well," said Jenny, "it's a long story. Let's just say money was found. And we have a boss who is very good at getting funds out of our organization's sponsors."

"You mean the NATO countries?"

"Maybe," said Jenny, intoning the final vowel almost to the point of sarcasm.

"He's very good at playing them off each

other," said Kiki. "It's an art. Like being a successful game show host. If somebody has a grudge against somebody else they can be convinced to pony up a bunch of cash."

"That's absolutely ridiculous," said Hawthorne. "They must go through so much wasted money."

"You should see our headquarters. The money they lavished on it."

"Didn't you guys blow up a building about a couple of months ago? That was what the rumors were."

Kiki and Jenny looked at each other. "Rumors," said Jenny, "that will never be confirmed."

"Anyway," said Hawthorne, "usually my job is to recruit people. And run them. They think it's cheaper to hire me temporarily. Because so many of their agents were getting compromised in Europe. When a government employee got found out, you've got to ship them back to Washington. And give them a job working a desk somewhere. For life. The accountants figured out it's cheaper to put me on contract and pay me scads of money. But the only catch is—"

"What's that? No one respects you?" said Jenny

"I don't have an office."

"You do everything out of the back of your car?"

"I'm very mobile. I do a lot of moving around."

"What's you disguise? Traveling salesman?" said Jenny.

"Maybe," said Hawthorne. "The bottom line is that the CIA stuff is usually pretty good. But not always. I do some work for Canadian intelligence when times get lean. And sometimes for NATO. As long as it's in sight of the five eyes. Digby phoned me up and asked me to get a hold of you two."

"Why? He didn't trust me?" asked Jenny.

"I don't need to get into a jurisdictional fight. I'm just saying there were concerns that you two might get involved with the local police. Turns out you did. So I'm here."

"I don't understand. You look like a guy who has no loyalties whatsoever," said Kiki.

"My loyalties are the same as yours," said Hawthorne. "Money. That's the thing you've got to understand. In the future all secret agents will basically be working for somebody else's dreams. Or revenge strategies. And we're milking them because they'll spend good government funding just to get back at people. Or steal somebody's secrets. So they can lock them in a vault."

Kiki nodded. "That's what the Chinese do."

Jenny rolled her eyes. "That's a totally different ballgame. They think they're getting ahead gathering all these secrets. Maybe they're hoping to run an extortion scheme."

"The bottom line is that your friend here, Ridley, has quite a history. He's the real issue."

"Of course he is," said Kiki. "He used both me and our organization."

"Well, that's another reason why Digby was encouraged—" Hawthorne's use of the word implied Digby's hand had been forced— "to hire me. Because of my level of trust in the CIA."

"You mean you're not tracking our emails?" said Jenny.

"Of course we're tracking your e-mail. But you know that's NSA not CIA. I'm here in case anyone tracks dirt onto U.S. soil. From Canada."

"I thought that was the secret service?"

"Well, I may have to hand some files over. Eventually"

"But we've already lost these guys." Jenny stabbed at a piece of lettuce with her fork. "While we were in jail. They're gone. They could be anywhere."

"We know exactly where you're friend Ridley is going."

"Oh really?" said Kiki. "Where?"

"Obviously he's going to California."

She rolled her eyes. "And what makes you so sure of that?"

"Because we intercepted some e-mails. We know exactly where he's going to be for the next three days."

"And where is he right now?"

"We theorize he may try, in the next few hours, to cross the border. We'll get him then."

"You theorize?" Kiki wasn't convinced. "I'm telling you I had a conversation with their guy. That's probably typed in his—"

"No," said Hawthorne. "Leave it to me. He's going to California. That's where these drones operate out of. Most of them. Edwards Air Force Base."

"He's not—"

"I'm sure this guy acted like he was spilling the beans. Or on an ego trip of some sort. But in reality, it's highly unlikely he'd confess his whole plan to you."

"Listen," said Kiki. "I was talking to the guy Ridley's with. He tried to kill both of us. But before that he started asking questions."

"What are you trying to say?"

"The bottom line, is he's not going to California."

"Okay. So where's he going?"

Kiki had no answer for that.

"You want me to think that someone who tied you up and tried to assault you is more reliable than our security analysts?"

Kiki took a swig of beer. "Yes. Because he had nothing to lose. He expected me to be dead."

"Well, I'll pass that on. Anyway, tomorrow. Digby asked me to get the two of you to Trudeau Airport. They'll be flying in around one o'clock. So no misbehaving? Okay?"

"Why would we misbehave?" said Jenny.

Hawthorne looked at them warily. He was about to reply when the waitress arrived with their plates.

After dinner they had a few more drinks then went back to their rooms. Jenny's was the first stop. "I'll see you later," she said.

"How come you couldn't get our rooms side by side?" said Kiki.

"I don't know. Someone booked the room in the middle."

Jenny said goodbye and closed her door. Hawthorne saw Kiki to her room.

"Well, I guess this is good night."

"Yeah. I mean, uh, how were things back there? Just between you and me, how dangerous do you think these people are?"

"They were going to kill me," said Kiki.

"Is there anything else I can do to make you feel better? I am a trained psychologist, you know." Hawthorne took her hand.

"I don't think—" she retracted her hand— "you need to do anything. Good night, Mr. Steele. If that is your real name."

Kiki closed the door. After washing her face she started to undress. She had only her underwear. Dirty underwear.

She had just pulled up the bedspread when she heard a knock at the door.

CHAPTER 10.5

Kiki paused at the door for a moment before opening it. The dead bolt was secure. She looked though the peephole and saw Hawthorne. "I need to get to sleep."

"Look, wait— hear me out. Open the door. Please?"

After a moment's hesitation she complied. He had a package in his hand. "What is that?"

"Well, I still have a couple more questions."

"Can we not discuss this in the morning?"

"Yes, but I brought a couple things. For you—" He squeezed through the door and lay a square package and a grocery bag on a nearby table. "I have the finest Blanche de Chambly. That's beer. And a couple of glasses."

"Why are you bringing this over now? I'm tired. I've been through a lot."

"Just give it a try. It's very good."

"Please it's—"

"A couple glasses won't hurt you. And," he passed the box in his left hand to her, "this is some ladies underwear. I gave some to Jenny before dinner. I figured you might still be, uh, roughing it."

"How kind of you... you don't expect me to wear this while we're talking, do you?"

"No," said Hawthorne. "I brought it because I know you left your luggage back in Quebec City. It couldn't hurt to have fresh panties, right?"

"Yeah. That reminds me—I still haven't paid that hotel bill."

"It's been taken care of. Something else I was kind enough to do. Your luggage is still there, however. If you were wondering."

"Oh, I wouldn't worry about that."

"Now, since I've been such a wonderful errand boy," he said, "would you mind sitting down for a couple minutes?"

"Fine," said Kiki.

He poured out the beer. She took a sip. "This is pretty strong stuff."

"It won't kill you."

"You want me to confess to something?"

"I don't want any confessions."

"You said you were a psychologist."

"I have a doctorate in psychology. But I can't prescribe drugs."

"Why?" she said. "Does that make you good at interrogation?"

"I've been known to get information. I need to know why Ridley wanted you to join him."

"Why? I don't know why."

"Okay, let me phrase it another way—"

"Are you trying to say that I'm under suspicion? That I'm working both sides?"

"No," said Hawthorne. "You've made your decision. It's that you're very new. Some of us want to know who we're dealing with."

"Well," said Kiki, "what do you want to know?"

"Why he asked only you. And no one else."

"I think he might still love me. Our relationship had been, um, intense. To a point. I bet he really thinks what he's doing is right. Even if it's for the wrong reasons."

"Do you still love him?"

There was an awkward pause. "I don't know if I ever loved him. But I know what you're getting at," she said.

"Really?"

"You want to know if you should let me continue. Me and our group. Or just let the CIA and secret service take over, right?"

"If someone has stolen a drone, we want to make sure we get it back. Sometimes we don't have the resources to do it. The question is, do you?"

She smiled. "You do whatever the hell you want. Am I going to have to put up with this line of questioning for the rest of the night?"

"No, that's not what I meant." He stood up. "I should go."

Kiki stood up as well. "It's not that— it's just—"

Hawthorne leaned in and awkwardly kissed her. She pushed him away. "Look—" he was so childlike. So awkward. This was the man they'd sent? "I don't care what you're trying to do. I'm not interested in you."

"Yeah," he said. "I shouldn't be doing this. I'm probably just jealous. It's a bad idea." He turned around and got ready to go.

Kiki looked at him as he walked out. He paused when he got the door open. "One more thing. What did you think when you found out I was following you?"

She looked at him. Staring. Their gaze held. He moved in closer. And kissed her some more. She didn't stop him this time.

He just kept going. Again and again. She felt his tongue move into her mouth. She really wanted to continue. It must have been the alcohol that had gotten them this far. She was very excited.

Then something in her realized this was not going to go over well. Maybe it was some sort of reverse honey trap. He'd already got her to talk about her relationship with Ridley. If they stuck together perhaps he'd get even more information.

She pushed him away. "No," she said. "I've got to get to sleep."

"Are you sure? I'd really like to—"

"Go. I know karate. I'll break your arm if you don't leave right now."

Hawthorne moved away. Slowly at first. Then scooted out of the room in embarrassment.

God, she though, these people are insane.

She went to bed. Set the alarm for eight o'clock the next morning. She drifted off to sleep quickly. No doubt the effects of the Blanch de Chambly.

SMASH!

Something woke Kiki. Someone was screaming. She looked at the alarm clock. It was two-thirty in the morning. A car door slammed. What the hell was going on?

CHAPTER 11.1

Kiki rushed to the door. In slippers and underwear. For a moment she almost stopped in embarrassment, wearing nothing more than a bra and panties.

Another scream.

She flung open the door. To see Jenny being forced into the back of a blue Dodge SUV. As Kiki got closer she saw the face of a man—Giancarlo. Still in full priest outfit.

He turned and saw her. Raised a pistol in her direction.

BANG! BANG!

Kiki got out of the way just in time. He was

a terrible shot. Missed her by a wide margin. She took cover behind a nearby truck. Giancarlo got into the driver's seat of the Dodge and put the car in gear.

Hawthorne was already out of his room. He ran across the parking lot and got into his Taurus. Kiki wrapped on the windshield as he backed out the car. He unlocked the door and she got in. They were both still in their underwear. Something that distracted her for only a moment before she heard the tires of Giancarlo's truck. Squealing out of the parking lot.

"Come on, hurry up. He kidnapped—"

"I know. Why did he pick Jenny?"

"I don't know. The first room he came across, maybe."

"I though you people knew how to defend yourselves."

"We do. He must have hit her with a taser or a tranquilizer dart."

"That explains the struggle. It takes a while for those things to kick in, you know."

"I know."

Giancarlo's SUV was already out of the parking lot, speeding away on the country road.

Kiki looked at him. "What are we going to do?"

"I don't know. Have you got a gun?"

"No," she said. "You don't have one?"

"Uh, no," said Hawthorne.

"Why not? I thought you were a secret agent?"

"Canada's border services are very strict about things like that."

"Unbelievable. This is what you get for going freelance, isn't it?" she said.

Hawthorne floored the accelerator. "Any faster and he's gonna go off the road," he said. "There's no way he can survive it."

"Just remember, my friend's in there too, okay? Before you start chasing and smashing into things."

"I know." He got the Taurus as close as possible to the back left corner of the SUV.

BANG!

He smashed the side of the Dodge. Just behind the left rear wheel.

"That's not going to do it."

Hawthorne swerved, recovered, and accelerated. Giancarlo was flooring it. The Taurus was no match for the SUV. He swerved into the oncoming lane, and got close to overtaking Giancarlo. "I've got to get his wheel, that's the only way."

BANG!

Hawthorne hit one more time against the

side of the Dodge. Before headlights appeared in front of them.

On the two-lane road he had no place to go. He pulled back. A small light truck passed by at the last minute.

"What are you trying to do?" said Kiki. "Kill us?"

"I'm trying to get him off the road." The forest that shrouded the road opened up to fields. And an intersection up ahead. One more time Hawthorne gunned the engine and swerved for a hit.

He missed.

It was getting more difficult. It seemed Giancarlo was catching on to what he was doing.

They ascended a crest. One more time Hawthorne slammed against the back corner of the SUV. It fishtailed out. And swung around to the left. Giancarlo hit the brakes. The Ford Taurus shot ahead. Hawthorne slowed, watching in his rearview mirror. The hunter was now the hunted.

Kiki looked back and saw Giancarlo's headlights shining in her face. "We have to go back around."

"Don't worry. I'm just going to block the road." He parked the Taurus right over the centerline.

BOOM!

The SUV collided with the rear corner of the sedan. It hurried past, spinning the car around. Kiki slammed into Hawthorne's shoulder. "You thought this piece of junk would stop him?"

"Look, it worked in training," he said

"God, you're going to get us killed."

Hawthorne gunned the engine. They were approaching a major highway intersection. "You can make it. We can do this."

There was a stoplight up ahead. Giancarlo gunned it through. Hawthorne pursued. Kiki looked to her left—

"Stop—Stop—"

At the last second Hawthorne saw it too. A huge pulp truck heading right for them. The green light was his.

Hawthorne swerved to the right. Into the ditch. The car couldn't handle the steepness of the embankment. It rolled onto its side.

Kiki looked around. They were both okay. The car was horizontal.

Hawthorne released his seat belt and rolled onto her.

"Jesus," she said. "You're going to crush me."

"Don't worry." He got his door open. The passenger side was now the floor. Hawthorne got out and Kiki followed.

She watched helplessly as the SUV trailed off in the distance.

CHAPTER 11.2

The car passed through Montreal's northern suburbs.

Hawthorne was at the wheel, driving Kiki to Trudeau Airport. He'd already switched cars. Again. Another Ford. This one was newer, though.

"You know," he said, "I should be thankful. Now I can charge a new car to the government. You really are a one-woman doomsday machine."

"Look, it's not my fault. Trouble goes with the territory."

"Yeah, well, we're lucky to be alive." Hawthorne pulled into the drop off lane on the arrivals level. "This is where I get off the Kiki Claymore roller coaster ride."

"Really? You're just going to leave me here?"

"Why? Are you disappointed?"

She looked at him long and hard for a moment. He reached over and tried to kiss her. She pushed him away.

"Not until you learn to drive better," she said.

"Fine. Say hello to Digby for me, will you?"

He drove off. Kiki wandered into the arrivals terminal and sat down. Ten minutes later Digby and Tatyana appeared. Digby was not in a good mood. "So, what's going on?" said Kiki.

He shot her a look that made the smile disappear from her face. "I've spoken to the sergeant—" she began.

"No," said Digby, waving her off like he was swatting a fly. "I talked to the police in Tremblant, Quebec. They know what we're dealing with. The hotel incident is going to be logged as a break in. Not a missing persons case."

"What you mean? I thought you wanted us to liaise with local authorities."

"I did. But this is causing way too much heat. We're in real trouble here, you know. You have no idea the crap I've had to go through in the last two days. I've dealt with no less than four local police forces. It's like you leave a trail of destruction everywhere you go."

"Don't worry," said Tatyana. "He's just been having a bad week. That's what happens when we do our jobs properly. It means he has to stop drinking and pay attention."

"Enough."

Tatyana rolled her eyes. "You're hung over from the flight, are you not?"

"I had a few drinks. To make sure I got my beauty sleep," he said.

"Great," said Kiki. "You're hung over and going to take it out on the rest of us." She looked around. "I thought Tin Man was coming?"

"He is," said Digby. "He's bringing the car around."

Kiki shot him a confused look. "You know I could have picked up a rental before you got here."

"No," said Tatyana. "This you just have to wait and see. He brought his van."

"He brought the same van he was using last time? In Amsterdam?"

"Oh no," said Digby. "This is a new one. He has no less than five. One for each major continent. He gets them shipped around on the back of a flatbed truck. Here he comes now."

Up to the passenger pickup area rolled a gigantic recreational vehicle. It was top of the line, too. And brand new.

Kiki turned to Tatyana. "You've got to be joking. Is this, like, our new disguise?"

"What do mean?" said Digby.

"Well, obviously nobody will think we're

secret agents. They'll assume we're senior citizens. I thought the whole point of us being here was to pursue somebody. Unless you're hoping the opposition will surrender out of frustration. Because they'll be stuck in a traffic jam. Caused by this thing."

Digby glared at her. "This is top of the line surveillance equipment. You have no idea how we work, do you?"

"Yeah," said Tatyana dryly. "This is crucial."

"Well..."

They piled into the RV.

Tin Man was in geek heaven. "Look at this thing. It's got four beds. I spent months designing it. Thank god you decided to get on that plane."

"What you mean?" said Kiki. He was so chipper.

"If you hadn't taken that flight to Canada I might never have been able to drive this thing. We have at least half a million dollars in surveillance equipment here. And a Jacuzzi."

"Isn't that just peachy." Kiki turned to Digby. "Where are we going? We need to find Jenny."

"I know," Digby said, taking a seat in the wrap around dinette booth. "But first we have to have a discussion about following orders."

Tatyana got in the driver's seat and they got underway.

Tin Man sat down next to Kiki. "Can I see your phone?"

"Sure. Me and Jenny tried to send you a bunch of stuff."

"I got some of it. But I really need to hook it up physically. To one of my machines here."

She dug through her purse. After an anxious moment she produced it.

"Now," said Digby, pouring himself a glass of cola and rum, "I admire you composure under pressure."

"I know how to stay calm." She looked at his drink. "You know it's not even lunch time yet?"

"I'm still on Amsterdam time. Besides, I'm dehydrated from the airplane." He took a gulp of his drink. "We have to have a discussion about how you behave. And which orders you take. I already have one agent kidnapped. I don't want that to happen twice."

"I can't control what the bad guys do."

"The opposition would have a harder time kidnapping if you picked places a bit more out of the way."

"I didn't suggest the hotel. Mr. Steele, who you hired—"

"Mr. Steele is an idiot." Digby put down his drink. "I had to resort to him because you chose the wrong place to go on a camping vacation. And don't trust anything he's saying either. I depend on you to pick the location. You should have known better." He reached over to the mini-fridge. Grabbed an ice cube tray. "Found a place near a police station. Or at least some lodgings near interference. Like heavy traffic. Some level of security. Not a Motel Six in the middle of the wilderness."

"Maybe you should give me a course on how to check for these things."

"Yeah. That's an excellent idea. We'll deal with that later."

"Besides, we were tired," she said.

"Any hotel is vulnerable," said Tin Man, "if you don't have enough people with you."

"Yeah, well..." Digby wasn't convinced.

Tin Man sat down next him. "It's true all of this is a Christmas pudding of foreign services. All refusing to coordinate. If it weren't for Kiki. Would you expect Spain, Germany, Canada, and the U.S. to all work together with such speed?"

"Well, maybe not," said Digby. "The bottom line—orders are orders." He took another gulp of his drink. "In the face of danger I like my agents to sit back and take a few sips of common sense."

"The question is," said Kiki, "whether we go after Jenny or Ridley. Giancarlo may have killed her by now."

"Yes, I know."

"So what are we gonna do?"

"We're going to go and get her."

"Where is she?"

Digby looked up. "Tin Man? Where is she?"

"I don't know. We haven't seen the signal yet today. But I bet I know where he's taking her."

"Where's that?" said Kiki.

"Don't worry. Sit back and enjoy the ride."

CHAPTER 11.3

"Your phone," said Tin Man. "Can you connect it to the computer there?"

Kiki grabbed a cable. A whole section of the trailer was devoted to a workstation with a bank of monitors. And blinking lights. Lots of them. "How big is this machine?"

"Oh, it's enormous," he said. "It takes up half the weight of the RV."

"For one computer?"

"That's how powerful it is. The only one like it. In the whole world. I'll be able to decode practically anything."

Half an hour later Kiki came back and checked in with him. "We should arrive in downtown Montreal soon. How are things going with my phone?"

"I'm having some difficulties."

"As in?"

"You scanned two hard drives, right? There were things that were missing?"

"Yeah. There were four hard drives in total."

"Well, we've only got half of it. It's not decoding particularly well. Everything has some strange sort of encryption on it. That's the machine's problem, not mine. Nonetheless, it's taking a long time. And I'm not happy with the packages I've been able to extract."

"How come?"

"It's strange. Not like anything I've ever seen." Tin Man looked at his watch. "And it's almost tea time. That's the worst part of it."

"Can you track Giancarlo's phone?"

"Oh, I thought Hawthorne would have tried that."

Kiki shook her head. "You'd better take care of it."

Another program popped up on Tin Man's screen. Several lights flickered. "Let's see, I think we have a record of Giancarlo's cell." A map appeared with GPS coordinates. "We can roll back through his location history."

He zoomed in until the map covered only southern Quebec. A scroll bar popped up. When it finished the computer had created an overlay with millions of dots.

"What am I looking at?"

"This is your phone. The blue dot in the middle. The red dots are all the cell phones active in the area. For the last three days."

"All this was recorded on my phone?"

"Yes." Tin Man clicked through a menu. "We're going to play this back. It's the entire geographical record. Every movement of every cell phone for the last seventy-two hours. When did you say you came into contact with him?"

"On the ferry. No," she corrected herself, "after the ferry. Across the river from Quebec City. In Levis."

The dots came alive, like a giant ant colony. "Here we go." He zoomed into the area around the ferry terminal. "I can see one signal. And then there was a car ride?"

"Yeah. But first the hotel."

Tin Man added some more parameters. "Then there was the cabin." More clicks and taps on the keyboard. "There's three things. We'll tie them together. Now, let's contact the satellite. Give it a few minutes. It should give us a location fix shortly."

"You can do all this? From my cell phone? Anywhere in the world?"

"Yeah. So can Apple. They do that. So does Google."

"Insane. And there's no laws we're breaking?"

"I don't deal with that. You'll have to ask the legal department."

"We don't have a legal department."

"There you go. No organization is perfect," he said.

A result flashed up. "Look at this. We have no idea where he is. Gone completely off the map. For the last twenty-four hours. And he's not using a phone issued by a major carrier. It's some sort of customized device. But," he clicked a few more buttons, "do you see that?"

"See what?"

"Look at the time signatures. Every day around four o'clock. He gets a phone call."

"Where from?"

"Finland."

"That's so weird."

"Yeah. Why would he be making a phone call to Finland?" Tin Man clicked through a few more screens. "Wait a minute. It's only being routed through Finland. It's coming from Sweden somewhere."

"Huh? That makes no sense. What dealings would Ridley and his gang have with Sweden? Nothing as far as I know."

"Very interesting. That reactor that we had trouble with? That was in Sweden, right?"

"Yeah."

Tin Man brought up some data. "But that was near Malmo. This is heading to Stockholm."

Kiki was growing impatient. "So, do you have any idea where he is?"

"No. But I've got a hunch." He called Tatyana on the intercom. "We should slowdown. Pull off at the next motorway rest stop."

"Why?" she said.

"There's no point in driving any farther. If we're going in the wrong direction."

"Okay."

Ten minutes later they were stopped outside an A & W off the Decarie Expressway.

Tin Man was glued to his monitor in anticipation. "And any second now—"

"What is his actual phone number?" said Kiki

"This is it, right here."

"So I could actually call him?"

"That's probably not the best idea."

"We're just going to wait until he calls somebody?"

Tin Man's display flashed. "His phone

just went on. It looks like he's going to get a text message or something." A scroll bar appeared. It said 'Tracking—77%'. Then the connection dropped. "Or maybe not. His phone is off again."

Half an hour later Tin Man yelled to her. "Kiki, get over here. Now." Everybody huddled around the monitor.

"You said this thing is going to work, right?" said Digby.

"It better work," said Tin Man. "It's interrupting tea time."

"What now?" asked Tatyana.

"We wait. By the way," he looked up at her, "remind me to pick up some maple syrup before we leave Montreal."

"Of course."

"Here we go. He's on. We can track him. And—"

"And what?" said Digby

"Uh-oh." Tin Man scrolled through a line of text. "That was a really short phone call. Less than thirty seconds."

Kiki grabbed her phone. She punched in Giancarlo's number.

"What are you doing?" said Digby

"I'm calling him. You need him to stay on the phone longer, right?"

"That won't work. He's got some sort of

encoding on it. It's being bounced around like a ping-pong ball."

"Hello?" It was Giancarlo.

Kiki smiled. "Remember me? From the cabin. We were very disappointed that you decided not to consult us. Before you borrowed our friend Jenny."

"Listen," said Giancarlo, "I'm sick of dealing with you. I'll kill her if you don't stop tracking me immediately."

"Why? You could have killed her in the hotel."

"I want to make sure you get the message."

"No, you don't," said Kiki. "This is all a distraction. And for what?" She looked over to Digby. He raised his arms questioningly. "Personally, I don't care. We want her back. Now."

"Three days." Giancarlo paused. Kiki heard footsteps. "In three days, if everything goes according to plan, she will turn up unharmed."

"What plan? What are you scheming?"

"I don't want to talk about this anymore. I have to go."

"No, wait. How do I know your not lying to us? We don't know you even have her."

"If you follow Ridley I'll kill her." He passed the phone to over.

"Hello?" It was Jenny.

"Where are you?"

"In the basement of the—"

"Stop. Three days." Giancarlo ended the call.

They murmured amongst themselves before Tin Man piped up. "Let's put the pieces together. They've got a drone. They've got a plan. And they've got us tied up here. God only knows what they're doing with the CIA. On the off chance the boys in Langley can get their brains wrapped around all this."

Digby cut in. "No one on the American side believes a drone has been stolen. You know that, right?"

Kiki shook her head. "But the police officer saw something—"

"No one has actually seen this thing take off or land. And I read a report that says it was an experiment. That went down in the ocean. I'm not denying what you say. But we've been here barely a day. It takes the boys in Washington longer than that to put two and two together."

"But we saw it—"

"It's an experimental aircraft. But it's not loaded with weapons. It's only been used for reconnaissance tests." Digby refilled his drink. "Right now we need to figure out where this guy is. What's his name?"

"Father Giancarlo," said Kiki.

"He couldn't hide just anywhere." Digby paused for a moment. He looked up at Kiki. "Why are you calling him father?"

"Well, that's how he introduced himself."

"Huh?"

"Well, he is a Catholic priest."

"What?" said Digby. "Why didn't you tell us?"

CHAPTER 12.1

"His real name is Farsil Singh." Digby was reading off his phone. "He's a Lebanese arms dealer who served with the Soviet army in Syria during the 1980's. He's also worked for Hezbollah. And is a proud defender of the Palestinian right of return. Of course that all went out the window in the late nineties when he started to disagree with the Hezbollah leadership. The last ten years he's gone freelance."

Tatyana grabbed a bottle of water. "Nobody wants to pay to hire killers full time anymore. So they just work for whoever. Maybe if you gave them real job security they wouldn't be busy robbing hotels. And blowing up cities."

"Good point," said Digby. "I'll take that under advisement. Now, last year he apparently took the identity of said Father Giancarlo. Who we have found out was actually an Italian clergyman. He died in the city of Eboli in southern Italy. Yet somehow it was never registered."

"Leave it to the Catholic church," said Tin Man, "to not keep its records updated."

"Well," said Digby. "It's possible they've heard of computers. So he takes this guy's stolen identity and uses it to pass through borders. Nobody really cares. Who's going to stop a priest?"

"Depends," said Kiki, "on what he's got on his computer."

"I mean who is going to stop one who isn't a pedophile." Digby turned to the workstation. "Tin Man, you've got that map?"

The lights dimmed. A screen rolled down over the windows opposite the breakfast nook. A projector switched on, displaying a duplicate of Tin Man's display. Digby operated a remote cursor with his phone. "Here is a basic map of Montreal. And this is the area we believe the target is located. Somewhere in the southern half of Montreal Island. Assuming our intelligence is correct. And it very likely is. He only could have gone—" Digby turned to Tin Man— "How far could he have gone?"

"He could have gone anywhere within twelve hundred miles. Assuming he didn't hit an international airport or a train line. No boat can travel fast enough to get substantially far away in seventeen hours."

"Exactly," said Digby. "Unless he snuck aboard a boat. In which case the long distance charges would have to go through a satellite router."

"How can you be sure?" said Kiki. "What if he wasn't in cell phone range?"

"The man has a plan," said Digby. "He wouldn't risk losing contact with the coach when all the bases are loaded. Anyway, the satellite router would have revealed itself. He's probably still in the area."

"What if he took her over the border?" and Kiki

"What?" said Digby. "In the middle of the night? Where do you think they are? Buffalo?"

"I'm just saying. It's not impossible."

"Yeah, I don't think this guy's going to all that much effort," said Tatyana. "Too much hassle. Especially when you've got a major city to hide out in. And a clever disguise."

Digby brought up a list of churches. "Tatyana has called around to various rectories looking for Giancarlo. No one seems to have heard of our man. But we did find out that someone has rented a room in the basement of the Notre-Dame cathedral. For storage. And study."

"Wait a minute," said Kiki. "That's right in the middle of Old Montreal."

Digby looked at her blankly. "Yeah? So what?"

"I thought we were secret agents? Secret. As in, not being seen by people?"

"Right. Sure."

"Parking a mobile home. On a warm summer night. In the middle of Old Montreal? Not the best way to stay secret. It gets crowded there. Tourists. Police. Especially if our man here has a gun and starts firing."

Digby nodded. "That's a good point. That's why you two are going in through the basement."

Tatyana glared at him. "The basement?"

"We've found two possible entrances. Pull them up, will you, Tin Man." A floor plan of the cathedral appeared on screen.

Tin Man turned to the girls. "We don't exactly know the layout because this is the digitized version," he said. "So it could have changed."

"Digitized version?" said Kiki.

"It's a little old."

Tatyana turned to Tin Man. "When are these plans dated?"

"1917."

"You can't be serious." Kiki shook her head.

"Don't worry about it," said Digby. "We're going to give you a gun."

"You're going to give her a weapon?" said Tatyana. "Oh, great. Just wonderful. Now I'm really fearing for my life."

Digby got out a highlighter tool and drew a path on the floor plan. "One person will go through this building. Two doors to the left. There's a tunnel leading from the basement. The other person will approach from the exact opposite direction."

Digby cleared his throat awkwardly. "Through a subterranean connection point."

"I don't want to go through the sewer," said Kiki.

"You're not. Tatyana is."

Tatyana's eyes widened. "What?"

"Don't worry. We're going to park over a manhole. This vehicle has a trapdoor. It's really remarkable. We'll lower you right down on a winch. Don't worry. It'll only smell bad for a couple of meters. The connecting door is close by. You'll be fine. A quick skooch through the catacombs and you're in."

"I'm not going into the sewer."

"There are catacombs in there. It's going to be historic. You know, like Indiana Jones and—"

"No way. I'm going through the front door."

"People will see you."

"I don't care. Find me a basement door."

Tin Man moved his cursor over the screen. "There are entrances here, and here."

"Good," said Tatyana. "I'm going that way. And what exactly are you guys going to be doing?"

"We'll be topside. Waiting for you to bring him in."

"Bring him in? What?" said Kiki. "Is he going to join us in the Winnebago?"

"Those are good questions," said Digby. "When we've established that he's our guy, Canadian Security has allowed us to use one of their offices. By the airport. Usually they use it to stop gypsies. And refugees. But in this case they're going to let us do our business there."

"And what if he gets shot or killed?" said Tatyana.

"Don't let him."

"These things happen," she said.

"Don't," said Digby. "Our number one priority is to keep him alive. Why? Because of all the crap that happened last week. I need someone to vouch that what we're doing isn't completely illegal. Even if we solve this mystery, we're still going to need someone to go before the Canadian and American governments. Show them what we did was worthwhile. I want to parade him in front of the committee back in Amsterdam."

"And if he dies?" asked Kiki.

"If he dies, all of us might end up going to jail."

CHAPTER 12.2

"What is with your friends?" said Giancarlo. "I tell you, this girl, Kiki— she never gives up."

"That's because she knows something called loyalty."

"And what about you? Do you stand by your organization at all costs? No matter how stupid the order?"

Jenny smiled. "The guy, Ridley, you've put all your trust in? He used to work with me. And he was a rat."

"Who are you talking about, The Zebra?"

"No, Ridley. Who's The Zebra?"

"It's not important. He's probably dead by now."

"He is dead. I saw it."

Giancarlo looked off into space. "It was so easy to take you from the room, you know."

"You used a stun gun." Jenny watched Giancarlo turn away. Even so she caught a glimpse of dismay on his face. He was having doubts about his cohorts. He didn't trust them. "What are you planning?" she said.

Giancarlo paused before turning around. "I want to know about Ridley. What's your opinion of him?"

"You mean you don't know?"

"I'm just one person. In a far bigger plan."

"To do what?"

"Nuclear things. That's my specialty. That and guns."

"You know how to kill people?" said Jenny

"Yeah."

"You want to show me your gun?"

"I don't think so. I'm going to be kind to you. I don't want you to cause any trouble. I'd like to get you something for dinner. What would you like? What is this food they have here? Poutine? It's delicious."

"Actually, a bagel would be nice."

"Why? Montreal is known for its bagels?" said Father Giancarlo.

"Oh yeah. They don't compare to New York. But they're really good."

"Ah, New York. You better get used to the Montreal variety."

Jenny leaned back in the chair. "So what is your plan, anyway?"

"Well," said Giancarlo, "it's Armageddon. But my job's done. I've already gotten paid. This is just a favor from me."

"What?"

"Kidnapping you. I didn't really want to do it. I think you're wonderful."

"This is bullshit," said Jenny. "You people don't know what you're doing."

"Oh?"

"Your plan is in shambles. And you hired a guy who just betrayed the only person he ever loved. And the only organization he's ever known."

"Really?"

"And you think he's going to go through with what he promised? He might betray all of you if we get to him."

"You need to have faith in people."

"You know Kiki? The girl you were talking to in the cabin? She pointed out something interesting to me."

"What's that?" he said.

"That you guys figured out everything.

Except you made one assumption that's completely wrong."

"What?"

"You never expected to get caught."

Giancarlo smiled. "You can't stop us. The plan—even I don't know all of it. That's the genius of this operation."

"What do you mean the whole plan?"

"I mean this stage. The airplane. That drone. That's just one small part."

"Huh?"

"Yeah, it's going to take place all over the world." Giancarlo took out his wallet and fingered through his bills. "Anyway, I'll get you something to eat. I'll even buy you some beer. To make you happy. But if you try to kill me, I'll shoot you. I've electrified the doors. You'll never get out. Unless you want ten thousand volts running through your feet." He put his hand on something in the corner. It looked like a space heater. Giancarlo flicked a switch. It made an odd hum. "See this device? Over here?"

"What is that?"

"It's a kind of battery. But it's been modified. To send a current all though the room. It's highly localized—from your chair you won't be electrocuted, but if you move towards the door... it's curtains. The current will jump. Arcing through the air."

"That's not possible. Oxygen is a poor conduit for electricity."

"This is different. It uses the metal in the walls and the floor."

Jenny looked around. The place looked like a dungeon. Old stone. With metal girders on the windows and doors. It felt like she was in some sort of medieval castle. "You would seriously do that? You'd kill me?"

"You have to remember something," said Father Giancarlo. "I'm just as much stuck here as you are."

CHAPTER 12.3

Digby and Tin Man dropped Tatyana and Kiki at separate subway stations across town. This way they'd approach old Montreal from different directions. If one were seen, the other would still be free to operate. They were to convene in the church basement. Outside where they believed Jenny was being held. At eight fifty-three. The sun would be down by then. Making it easier for them to sneak around. Hopefully without causing too much disruption.

Kiki exited Place des Arms station and climbed the hill. She walked through the crowded square in front of the church. To a restaurant adjacent to the cathedral. She found her way to a staircase leading down to the washrooms. In the ladies room she found a door to a connecting passage.

As she sized up the exit she heard two people moaning. They were making out in the toilet stall next to her. How romantic. Then she heard some snorting.

Are they doing lines in there? Great. Back in Montreal, she thought, the Thailand of North America.

Kiki took out her keychain. With her skeleton key she got the door unlocked. Flicked on the lights. It was a storage room. But the doorway to the catacombs was now a solid wall. She closed the door behind her.

"Tin Man, where the hell am I?" she whispered

"You're in a storage room? It's right to your left."

"Yeah, but there's a wall of... something. It's brick. There's nothing here."

"All right. Here's what you're going to do. You see your keychain? There's a small grey fob on the end. Unhook it. It's a small cylinder. Looks like a bullet."

"Yeah. Got it."

"There's a cap at the bottom. Turn it to the left until it comes loose."

Kiki did. And saw a glimmer of goo expanding out of it. "There's a toothpaste-like substance—"

"Don't touch that. Use it to stick the fob against the wall."

She pressed it against the brick. It adhered easily. "Done."

"Good. Move to the other side of the room. As far away as possible."

"Why?"

"Get away from there. Now."

She ran across the room.

"Crouch down. Your back to the door. Cover your ears and close your eyes."

She did and—

KA-BOOM!

The whole restaurant shook. Upstairs the waitresses looked around at shocked customers.

Kiki examined herself. She was okay. Acrid smoke drifted up from the brick wall. "What the hell was that?"

"Plastic explosive."

"Everyone's going to know we're here." The smoke had cleared. She looked at the wall. "The brick work is still intact."

"Give it a poke and jump clear."

She pushed on one of the bricks and jumped back. Nothing happened.

CLINK CLINK CLINK...

The whole wall collapsed like a house of

cards. "I found a passageway." She made her way through.

Above ground Tatyana entered the front of the Notre Dame basilica. She walked past the pews. Acting like she owned the place. No one else was there except for a couple of people praying in the back. She walked off to the far right and found a door that led to a stairwell. Walked all the way down. At the bottom she entered a meeting room. The whole place was walled with stone. Beautiful. She walked over to the corner of the room to find what she was looking for. A handle in the floor.

She lifted it up to reveal a set of stairs. "I'm in," she said to her microphone.

"Good."

Downstairs Giancarlo was arguing with Jenny. "You wanna know?" he screamed.

"Yeah. Do it. Do it," she screamed at the same volume.

Giancarlo lowered his voice. "We're going to drop the big one on Boston. And that's just the start of the movie."

"Really?" she said, taunting him on with her grin.

"Because you know what? The whole of the press and the government. They'll be worried about that for a month. They'll be checking all the nuclear stockpiles. They'll have their military on high alert. And they'll never, ever see us coming."

"What are you going to do?"

"Oh, I can't tell you that."

"Sure you can. Why not?"

He smiled. "After that, you can put two and two together," said Giancarlo. "First we take Manhattan. Then the rest of America. And then the world will be on its knees."

"You're going to do all this with nuclear weapons?"

"No, silly. That's just the first stage. We've got even crazier things planned. Even if one of these plots gets screwed up, even if they stop us today, you can't stop the other parts. You know, we've got people everywhere."

"Who is paying for all this?"

"You're gonna laugh," he said. "You would laugh your ass off. Because they don't even know they're paying for it. You know when you make a donation?"

"A donation?"

Now Giancarlo was ranting like a madman. "Like a charity. It's like these U.N. people. They get all this money. For what? To embezzle at the local brothels. In parts of Serbia and Africa. That's all they're doing with the money. Squandering the funds set aside for food and bureaucracy. It's all corruption.

So what if we're being a little bit dishonest? Everyone else is."

Giancarlo started pacing. "Why am I doing it? Why is he doing it? Why is anybody volunteering their time? Some people want revenge. Other people want simplicity. What do you want? How about a bagel?"

"Yeah. I'm starving."

"I'll get you a bagel. Maybe I'll tell you the rest when I get back. But maybe I'm telling you too much. If I tell you too much, I'll have to kill you. You don't want me to do that. So don't ask so many questions," he said. "I like you. You're sweet, you know. Even though you tried to kick my ass up in that cabin."

He approached the electrical device in the corner. "Now, you be careful when this thing is on. There could be electricity all over the place."

"I got it," said Jenny.

"Don't try to scream, either. It's sound activated."

"I don't believe you."

"Well, you try it out when I'm gone," he said.

Giancarlo switched on the device. Then he locked the door and left.

He never saw Tatyana aiming a pistol at him.

CHAPTER 12.4

Tatyana's Walther K was nestled between two crates of holy water. Stacked against the sides of the long hallway that lead out to an exit on the far side of the cathedral. She watched in amazement as Giancarlo walked past, oblivious. The place wasn't so dark. His eyesight must've been pretty damn poor.

Across the hall, in an alcove, Kiki was crouched down. She motioned to Tatyana to come closer. Tatyana waited until she saw the door at the end of the hallway swing open. A burst of light from the room beyond illuminated the old stone passageway.

It shut with a heavy slam. The two of them scurried forward. The door was locked to Jenny's cell. Tatyana got out her keys and selected the skeleton.

CLICK-CLICK.

They swung the door open.

"Stop!" Jenny whispered as loud as she could. "There's a device in the corner that will electrocute all of us if you move."

"What do you mean? What is it?" asked Tatyana. "Tin Man, are you hearing this?"

"Yeah, what is the deal?"

"I don't know. I have no idea what that is. It's some sort of device." She turned to Jenny. "What does it do?"

Jenny explained how the electricity could arc.

"Oh, I've heard of this before," said Digby, listening in the RV. "This is a tough one. You know what you should do?"

In the basement Tatyana nodded as she took instructions. "Okay," she said. "All right. I'll do that. Only once though... sure... okay..."

Kiki looked up at her. "What should we do?"

"Hold on. Stand back. Jenny, can you turn the chair around?"

"Yeah, I can do that." She slowly wiggled the chair in the opposite direction.

"You want to keep your back to this."

"Okay."

Tatyana pressed against her earpiece. She nodded at Digby's instructions. "Okay." She took out her pistol. "I'm doing that now."

She aimed toward the device.

But something caught her eye.

She lowered her gun and walked toward the contraption.

"What are you doing?" said Kiki.

Tatyana reached down and yanked the

device's electrical cord out of the socket. "Seems pretty safe to me." She turned to Jenny. "You spent the last ten minutes frightened to death by a de-humidifier."

Jenny looked over. "What the hell?"

Tatyana walked though the room. "No arcing here." She looked around for other booby traps. "Look how thick these walls are. It's like we're in a dungeon."

"Fantastic," said Jenny.

In the RV Tin Man shook his head. "That was your suggestion?"

"Look," said Digby, "it's experience. Allows you to adapt to any situation."

"Right."

Tin Man felt something. A pen laying on the counter in front of him slid over onto the floor. "What's going on?" The next to go was his empty coffee cup. "Is there an earth-quake?"

Digby's chair was rolling backwards. "The parking brake." He ran to the driver's seat. "Oh no. It's far worst than that."

He burst out of the RV and walked around the front. He confronted an obese French Canadian tow truck driver.

"Hey, listen—you can't be doing this here."

The French Canadian guy looked at him blankly. "No speak English," he said and pointed up to a sign. Then he pointed down to the curb, painted in red.

"No, see, you don't understand. I'm an American. Working for—"

"American?" The truck driver laughed. "I love Americans." He rubbed his thumb against his fingers. "Have money."

In the dungeon Tatyana was struggling to get Jenny freed.

"What do you mean? It's a pair of handcuffs," said Jenny. "They have a standard lock."

"Not this one," said Tatyana. "My key is designed for ninety-nine point nine per cent of the world's locks. And it's not budging. There's only two kinds of handcuffs. Which means there's only two kinds of keys in the entire world. What kind of person uses custom handcuffs?"

"Obviously these people did." Kiki looked around the room. It was completely barren. "Where would someone hide a small piece of metal in here? He must have them with him."

Tatyana scowled. "You mean we're going to have to go after that guy? Find him, and wrestle a set of keys from him?"

Kiki had an idea. She walked to the doorway. Right outside was a mat.

Tatyana pulled out her pistol. Aimed it at the handcuffs. "We don't have time."

"Wait," said Kiki. She lifted up the mat. "I found them."

"That can't possibly be the right set. No one would be lazy enough to leave them there."

Kiki walked over. Sure enough, they unlocked Jenny from the chair.

On the street Digby was paying off the tow truck driver. He piled up bills in the man's hand. Almost eight hundred dollars in twenties. He still wanted more.

Tin Man burst out of the RV. "They got her. She's free. They're ready to go."

"Great," said Digby. "Tell them we'll pull around in a second."

Neither of them noticed Father Giancarlo walking right beside the Winnebago. When he heard Tin Man's utterance, he paused. And turned right back the way he came.

CHAPTER 12.5

Giancarlo sprinted down to the catacombs. He was rushing towards the room when he saw the door ajar. Inside were the three girls. He quickly crouched down behind the crates of holy water. They had him at a disadvantage. What was he going to do? He reached around his back for the gun. He would wait here. The only way would be to kill them. One by one, as they left the room.

Kiki, Jenny, and Tatyana emerged from the makeshift dungeon. Not even noticing him in the shadows. He was ready. His finger unhooked the safety and was about to fire. When a sense of guilt came over him. Giancarlo may have been a sleaze and an arms dealer. But he didn't like to do the killing himself.

"Wait," he said. "Stop."

Kiki was the first one who saw the pistol.

"If you move any further," he said, "I'll have to shoot."

"No, you don't," said Kiki.

"Yes I do. Because I know your friends are outside. In the van, right?" Tatyana twitched at the mention. "You see, I know I'm not going to get out of this alive. To be extra careful, now, I have to shoot you. And I feel really bad. Unless you go back in there."

"No," said Jenny. "We're not. You're going to give yourself up."

"Don't make me do anything more." He moved up to Kiki and pressed the gun right against her head.

Kiki stared into his eyes. "Put the gun down."

"No, I'm not. And I don't care if you have to die. If I kill, I'll kill all three of you."

"You're not a killer," said Jenny.

Giancarlo's hand trembled. "I never used to be. But now I think... I might."

BOOM!

A gunshot reverberated off the stone hallway.

The sound was deafening. Kiki shut her eyes. She still felt the gun pressed against her forehead. Then the pressure lightened.

PLOP—

Giancarlo.

Kiki looked down. He'd been shot. The bullet expanded on impact. His chest was bleeding.

Digby stood up behind him, shotgun in hand. He had been crouched in the corner. Shot Giancarlo at just the right angle. The bullet had fired upwards and missed Kiki.

"You could have killed me," she said

"Hey," said Digby, "that guy was going to kill you, too. And that was a good shot."

"Yeah," she said, "thanks for aiming well."

"You're alive aren't you?" said Digby. "You should be so lucky. I just shot a man in the back. We're all a little guilty, aren't we?" He looked down at the bloodied Giancarlo. "Everybody's going to hate me, anyway. But

I'm still walking." He turned to Kiki. "And you're still walking. That's all that matters."

"This guy—" he motioned to Tatyana— "is he going to live?"

"He'll be fine," she said, examining his wound. "Too bad you didn't hit him on the side with the heart. But I'll bet he's got a collapsed lung." Giancarlo reached into his pocket and pulled out... something. He stuck it in his mouth.

"No!" yelled Jenny.

Giancarlo crunched down and swallowed rapidly. "You're not going to get me. I don't care."

"What is that?" Tatyana kneeled down and slapped him in the face. "What is it?"

"It's going to be a long trip to heaven. Watch out for McGraw's brother."

Five minutes later he was dead.

The police arrived. Digby spent the next two hours explaining himself to the officers and the church bureaucracy. Fortunately they were able to get out of there before the reporters arrived.

"Another place. Another trail of destruction," said Digby. They were back on the road in the motor home. "What did he say before he died? Watch out for his brother?"

"I figured that out," said Tin Man. "Vice-

Admiral McGraw is the head of the U.S. seventh army command. At a naval air station in Cape Canaveral."

CHAPTER 12.6

"Cape Canaveral?" said Kiki. They had headed back to a motel on the outskirts of Laval. Far from the luxury she'd experienced in Barcelona. But it had the advantage of being innocuous.

"I don't know," said Digby. "This whole thing is weird. How's Jenny doing?"

Tin Man turned to Kiki, looking for answers. "She'll be okay," she said.

Digby paced in front of the TV. "She'll have to go back to Amsterdam for a little while. Then she can take some time off. Down in Baltimore. I don't want someone freaked out on my team. She has time off coming up anyway." He got up and left.

A few minutes later Digby came back in the room. "I need to know more about this aircraft. It's time for me to go down to Florida and find out. You guys go on to California. Follow Ridley."

"How do you know he's going to California?" said Tatyana.

"We've gone through all the e-mail surveillance. Everything indicates that's his destination."

Kiki was frustrated. "But he's not going to California."

"It was in the report. Besides, Giancarlo could have been bluffing. Just like he was with Jenny's space heater."

"Why would he do that? It makes no logical sense."

"It's psychological warfare," said Tatyana. "These people are always trying to lay a false scent. People can be very convincing. You're not as good at spotting sincerity as you think."

"I'm telling you. Ridley, right now, is on his way down I-95," said Kiki. "Probably headed towards Florida. Can't you connect these things? That's where he's going."

Digby stopped pacing. "The e-mail trail these guys left says something else. That's what we professionals call evidence in this business."

"You said yourself they cover their tracks pretty well. You think they have the resources to kidnap a drone. But they don't have the ability to fake a trail of e-mails to com sec intelligence?"

"The com sec guys are top notch," said

Digby. "How the hell do you know better than them?"

"Because I know the guy. Something about this just doesn't feel right."

Digby headed for the door. "I don't know. You guys figure it out. In the meantime stay out of trouble. I don't want to hear about any more police showing up. Secret agents should stay secret. Otherwise, you're just an amateur detective." He slammed the door on the way out.

"What do we do now?" said Kiki.

"There's a secret on those hard drives," said Tin Man. "We'll do what most secret agents do."

"What's that?" said Kiki.

"We look through data. Meticulously." Tin Man paused for a moment. "And we wait."

CHAPTER 13.1

The RV pulled into the arrivals level of Trudeau Airport. Digby grabbed his laptop bag and a tiny suitcase. Kiki passed him his suit jacket. "Are you really going to Florida in a full three-piece suit and tie?"

"This is my flying gear. People need to know who's the boss."

"It's really hot down there, you know."

"Easily over a hundred in the humidity," said Tin Man.

"Look, I grew up in Arizona. I know these things. Don't worry about me." He turned around one last time before he departed.

"You guys will be safe to get down to California without me?"

"You're sending us on a wild goose chase," said Kiki.

Digby shook his head. "Believe whatever you like. This operation is not turning into chaos because of your hunches, okay?"

Everyone nodded.

"Arrivederci."

Once he was gone, Tatyana turned the RV south from the airport, towards the border with Vermont.

Kiki sat in the passenger seat for a while. "How long before we get there?"

"I'd say probably an hour. Ninety minutes, tops. Depending on traffic."

"And you're sure we'll be able to get this machine through?"

"I don't know. It shouldn't be a problem."

"I thought we had a special license we could flash. To get us through quickly."

"We did, but now that you've antagonized several police agencies, we're trying to go through the regular way. We're getting a bad reputation with border services and certain authorities. No one will be happy to see us."

"Why?"

"Your friend Hawthorne Steele told all his buddies."

"I hope I never see him again."

"I wouldn't bet on that. He's probably following you right now."

Kiki went to the back. Tin Man was working at his counter. "I think I figured out how this thing operates," he said, scrolling through code from the Daedalus.

"Really?"

"Well, it's quite dastardly. This main control circuit. These sorts of drones have their own artificial logic."

"Okay. What does that mean?"

"It means essentially this machine could fly on its own. It can make mission operation decisions. All by itself. There's already been a generation of these devices developed. The computer can select landing sites. Calculate whether their approaches are going to work. But this one is on a whole new level. They wanted to design this thing so that if a nuclear war broke out, it would follow its targeting orders no matter what."

"You mean this thing can be programmed to drop a bomb somewhere? And it will just go and do that? Without control or interference from a human being?"

"Basically, yes."

"That's a doomsday machine, isn't it?"

"Well, yeah. In theory. It could do that.

But lots of machines are the same. A ballistic missile, for instance. Or a smart bomb."

"Most missiles are operated by controllers, right? This thing could just fly anywhere and do anything it wants."

Tin Man nodded. "That is that danger. But the engineers put in some safety protocols. You said this thing was being stored in a hanger northern Quebec."

"That's right," she said.

He brought up a few schematics on his computer. "This is the model we're talking about. The one reported lost by the U.S. Navy. It's probably what you saw up there. It can take off and land anywhere. You can control its programming locally. But once it's in the air it will only receive instructions from the ground base station."

"Okay," said Kiki, more than a little confused.

"Otherwise, it will simply monitor local air traffic control. It will continue flying, invisible to radar. All the while avoiding the paths of other aircraft. It will fly at a cruising altitude of eighty-six thousand feet. Thanks to hyper-efficient engines that reduce the need for oxygen. And it's capable of flying even higher. This is just a rumor I discovered, but some say suborbital operations are possible."

"So it's a spacecraft?"

"This particular model has an experimental engine. That's why no one wants to talk about it. Whether or not it could make it to the edge of space, no one knows. But it was designed for that. So far they've only done preliminary testing."

"A flying bomb, basically."

"Yes and no, obviously. This particular model isn't equipped with armaments. But let's say you're the bad guys. And you want to launch it from somewhere. Because you've broken the coding. You want to crash it and kill a bunch of people. Well, there's a problem."

"What's that?"

"First of all, this is a surveillance drone. And it's an experimental aircraft. When this thing was captured it didn't have any equipment on board that could hurt anyone."

"That's a relief. So we don't have anything to worry about?"

"Well there's another hitch. It has an entire section here devoted to the hookup of a nuclear bomb."

"What?"

"We've been able to match intelligence reports from what Strobe was doing in Hamburg. Ridley obtained from him a very specific kind of nuclear weapon. That device, with a few modifications, is compatible with this drone's armament set up."

"So we're screwed?"

"Possibly, yes. I mean someone could potentially detonate this aircraft above a major city. Causing massive amounts of damage. Or fly it really low. That would be worse. Before it impacted the earth it would explode, kicking up a huge amount of radioactive dust."

"There's a third part to this, isn't there?"

"Yes. Your friend, Father Giancarlo. He's a nuclear engineer who's done extensive design work with compact nuclear arms."

"This is not good."

"It could be really, really bad. However, there is a bright side. When they built this thing they figured it might crash somewhere less hospitable. If the Russians or the Iranians captured it, the first thing they'd want to do is get it airborne. Maybe ram it into some enemy city. So the engineers built in a safety catch."

"What? A special key?"

"No, far better. It has a directional signal locator."

"Which means what?"

"You can't just feed it the correct coding. And then expect it to do what you want. You have to send the commands from the correct location. This is where it gets interesting. The communications array is designed to receive instruction from a place hard wired to that aircraft."

"Hard wired?"

"You have a radio in your house, right?"

"Well, actually—"

"Radios will pick up any broadcast signal. Transmissions meant to be received over a large-scale area. But this drone has a measurement device. It reads the amplitudes of the wave and its directionality. And the oscillations in the wave. It can tell, down to five hundred meters, where the signal has been generated. If the machine determines the instructions are not from the correct tower it's been encoded for, the aircraft is programmed to ignore those instructions."

"So what does that mean?"

"It means that if Ridley wants to control this thing—now that it's in the air—he has to go and find the corresponding locator beacon and broadcast from there."

"Is that difficult?"

"Well, no. The technology to take over a beacon and use it to broadcast a signal is fairly simple. I could teach a ten-year-old to do it. He'd just have to be at the physical location."

"But they don't just put locator beacons anywhere, do they?"

"That's the real issue now, isn't it?" said Tin Man. "He's got to get past all the security and everything. Which is probably on a military base. Then he'd have to scale a kind of tower. Or at least get to the ground station."

"That's impossible. There's no way he'll be able to do that."

"That's what I thought, at first. But after pondering what we've seen, I've come to realize there's another problem. With the security around the device."

"What?"

"Think about it. How they got the coding in the first place. Chances are, they have somebody working inside the base."

"You really think that's likely?"

"They're not doing this on their own. You can't just hijack a piece of military equipment. Not as a civilian. With an Interpol warrant out for your arrest. You need things like a military ID. Or a set of official orders. To get you through all the checkpoints. And he's probably already got them."

Kiki stood up. "Where do you think he's going?"

"I don't know. But I can make a guess. Tin Man pulled up a map on the computer. He's probably headed somewhere between Philadelphia and Grenada."

"Huh? Those two places are thousands of miles from each other."

"That's right. The good news is, he's probably in the United States. He won't want to cross any more land borders. Now that everybody's looking for him. Unless he has some sort of plane that he's chartered, but that's unlikely."

"I don't know. That looks like an awful lot of air bases."

"I agree. But I found something on those hard drives. That could be our ace. They've been using them to keep a record of Skype conversations. Literally hours of video. These guys are really paranoid. A regular bunch of Richard Nixons."

"You're joking."

"So that's what you've been doing? Watching TV? While we've been busting our asses to rescue Jenny?"

"Drinking tea. Watching telly. Looking for the conversation I'm about to show you."

"If it's incriminating, what do you think we should do?"

"Like every good sex tape," he said, "I'd post it on the internet."

CHAPTER 13.2

Ridley sat in his hotel room watching the free HBO. The one good thing that America had brought to the world. Pay television. He had settled in for the night and poured himself a vodka and tonic from the mini-bar. The presence of which was a complete surprise. He had no idea that a motel this cheap, just off the interstate, could possibly have such a sophisticated convenience. The place even had room service.

His phone vibrated. He picked it up. Expected to see another text from one of his cohorts.

It wasn't. It was Kiki.

How the hell had she got his cell phone number? Of course they could trace any phone. Data probably picked up at the abandoned mine. It was only a matter of deduction wasn't it? He had been sloppy. Forty dollars at an interstate truck stop would get him a new mobile. He had been in such a rush it hadn't occurred they'd be watching him. The only comfort he took was that all the incoming transmissions were coded. The only way Kiki could find him was if he replied to her.

He thought long and hard for a moment. An idea occurred to him. He could turn this lemon into lemonade.

Ridley looked at the text. "We're on to you," she wrote. "Before you make any more moves, you might want to watch this video. "

He clicked on the link. It was publicly viewable. A Skype conversation. In the main window was Giancarlo. He recognized the background—the hangar at the mine.

In the small corner of the screen was the video link from the other end. A man. Face obscured. By some sort of pixilation. It's like a goddamn Japanese porno movie, he thought.

"Everything is going fine," said Giancarlo. "I made it here without any hassles, but I think doing a few things differently—"

"Deal with it and stop complaining. Is everything ready to go for stage three?"

"Yes, but I'm worried about this person you set us up with."

"Who?"

"The Ridley character. He's too volatile. Too ambitious."

"But you met him twice."

"I've had time to think about it, over the last two weeks. He might have people on his tail."

"Who? The girlfriend? She won't be a problem."

"Her grandfather's been an operative. I've had dealings with him."

"Indirectly," said the pixilated man.

"Yes, but I gathered the opinions of some former colleagues. He was recently targeted with a successful erasure. The girl could have a grudge against us."

"But they can't possibly be connected."

"Of course not. But it's something to consider. You should really get me a picture of this girl. I should know everyone he was operating with before."

The pixilated man laughed. "You expect us to risk our cover? Our anonymity? For your paranoid preoccupations? There are thousands of people employed by that office. All across Europe. There's no way of keeping track of all of them."

"You must be able to find out if he was followed?"

"I'll look into it. No guarantees."

"I think we should kill The Zebra."

"Fine. He's simply muscle. Dispose of him as you wish. Once the aircraft is airborne." There was an awkward pause in the conversation. "There is nothing to stop us from getting rid of you, either."

"Oh, I am well aware of that. As long as you can cover the trail that leads to you. What about Ridley?"

"He's disposable as well. After this stage is complete. But until then, he's crucial. He's the one who set up the connection with South America."

"He did that through his old colleague. The one that died in Hamburg."

"Don't be hasty. He could be more valuable than he seems right now. Before you kill him, make sure you get my approval. Even with liabilities he continues to deliver benefits."

"If you insist."

"I do. Of course, in the long run he knows too much. To be allowed to stay alive."

The video ended there.

Another text from Kiki arrived. I hope you've watched it. We can always still be friends. You'll always be worth more to us alive.

He closed the computer. After three more drinks he went to sleep. Boozing himself into a shallow state of slumber. He woke hours later. The morning sun coming through a slit in the curtains. The alarm clock said six o'clock.

He grabbed his phone and sent Kiki a message.

No way.

CHAPTER 13.3

Kiki was already showered when she heard the knock at her hotel room door. It was Tin Man and Tatyana.

"You were right," said Tin Man. "He gave up his position. Just outside Philadelphia."

"You really think he'll stick around?" said Kiki.

"It's the best lead we've had so far. Maybe he had a change of heart."

"I don't believe that," said Tatyana. "Not for a moment. Anyway we have to get across the border. Who knows how long that could take?"

Five minutes later they were on the road. Tatyana was driving. Kiki in the passenger seat. "What do you think we should do?" Kiki said.

"Just be quiet. Everything will go fine. Don't worry about the border guards."

They crossed the border without incident. Tin Man's equipment was all welded inside reversible cabinets. That could be swung around to present a friendlier façade.

Kiki was impressed. "How did you hide all your stuff?"

"What do you think the cereal boxes are for?" He pointed up to the top shelf of the cabinet. "See all those tins up there? That's all our short range weapons and ammunition."

"None of this is actually food?"

"None of it," said Tin Man. He picked up a can with a Chef Boyardee label. "This looks like an ordinary tin of ravioli. Take a look at this." He turned it upside down a pressed his cell phone against the now upright bottom. The exterior of the can slid off, revealing a pair of communication headsets. "Devilishly ingenious, eh?"

Kiki was impressed. "You could get a lot of contraband across that border."

"I thought about it. I figured if NATO takes away our funding I could make a decent wage on the side."

They passed quickly through Vermont. Tatyana really gunned it.

"You should really slowdown, said Kiki. "Some of these redneck cops will stop you for ten clicks over the limit."

"I don't understand," she said. "I thought this was America. Land of the free."

"Yeah, but they're still trying to collect money. They'll see the out of state plates.

You'll be the first one they stop. Freedom comes at a price. Just under two hundred dollars."

Tatyana shot her a sarcastic grin and slowed down. After an hour up front, Kiki headed back.

"Well, you see, this is very interesting," he said, seemingly happy to have an audience. "There is a certain type of fuel. You can only get it in three places in the whole world."

"Really?"

"Yeah. It's not a normal kind of kerosene. This drone was designed to fly continuously for three days. There's no way to do that with conventional aviation fuel. Now, some of the time it's able to act like a glider, which conserves fuel consumption. But what they're using has a special kind of polymerase that channels through the ignition modules. In a repeated cycle. With a normal fuel, it reaches combustion and that's the end of the line. With this fuel it's recycled back to minimize the energy conversion. It lets go of only the slightest bit of energy as it passes through the engine and—"

"Ignition molecules?"

"It's a long story. Bottom line, the stuff is only made in three places."

"Which are?"

"Omaha, Munich, and outside Stockholm."

"So..."

"So it means that if we find your ex-boyfriend, we should ask him about those three places. This is where we should focus, in my opinion."

"I wouldn't mind going to Stockholm."

"Well, before that, we have to figure out where this thing is. I've done a bunch of calculations." He brought up a map on the screen. "This is where we were. The drone is probably flying around at a very high altitude. It isn't going north, it's going south, because that's where all the people live. Now if we believe Giancarlo—"

"Boston?"

"Exactly. Now if you put the drone in energy conservation mode I've calculated that it could stay circling above the northeast for up to six days."

"That's a lot of time."

"It is. These people really knew what they were doing. They must have someone on the inside. There's something else that is strange, too."

"Like what?"

"There's a whole bunch of coding on these drives. I've been going through it. Some of it is really, really weird."

"As in—"

"All these commands to quit the program. Stop it from doing things. I'd love to run it, but I'm missing parts of the execution line. I have the clues but no crossword. It's like an emergency switch. Bypassing the regular communications circuit."

"And you're telling me this...why?"

"Just be aware of it. Should something befall me."

"I doubt that will happen." Kiki looked around evasively. "Can I get your opinion on something?"

"Sure. Ask me anything. As long as you make me a cup of tea next time we're stationary."

"I guess that's fair enough."

"You have some sort of problem."

"I kissed someone."

Tin Man leaned back in his chair. "I knew it. I had a bet going on about this."

"What?"

"I know who you kissed."

"You do?" She looked away from him. "It's really embarrassing."

"There's no need to feel that way. At least three per cent of the population is like yourself."

"Huh? What are you talking about?"

"You kissed Jenny."

"Absolutely not. Jenny's a lesbian?"

"Well, we have no proof. But I have my suspicions. She shows no interest in going to bed with me."

"You're so sexist."

"Then why are you telling me your relationship troubles?"

"Good point. You see, there was a CIA agent."

"Uh-oh."

"His name is Hawthorne Steele."

"Oh, that guy."

"You know him?"

"No, but I've heard of him. He's been popping up the last couple of years. Back in the old days everyone was a public servant. It was all hush-hush, goody-goody. People dated each other if they worked for the same place. It was all very incestuous. But the company could be sure they had everybody's loyalty. Nowadays when you date someone in our business, you never know if they're plotting against you. And they probably are."

"I gathered that. He seemed to be trying to shake me down for information. Even as he caressed my... earlobes."

"Huh? What did you do? Put out?"

"I just sort of, you know, let him French kiss me."

"What? That's nothing. I thought this was going to be useful gossip. I have work to do, you know."

"Look, I was wondering how people feel about me having a relationship."

Tin Man looked at her blankly. "Let me put it this way. The last time you had a relationship with someone at work, they tried to hijack a nuclear power plant. And lay waste to a major northern European city. Don't expect the next time to be any better."

CHAPTER 13.4

Kiki pulled up to the hotel in a rented Ford Flex.

This was the first part of the plan. Tatyana and Tin Man had parked the RV across the street in an Arby's parking lot. It was hard to explain to Tatyana the particular American obsession with fast food. Even Kiki was amazed by the sheer variety of under priced and over-caloried restaurants in the suburbs of Virginia.

She got out and walked into the lobby of a Motel Six. They were only a few miles from the Pentagon. Which worried her. Someone might be following them. Or following Ridley. All they needed now was the lion's nest of American security to descend on him. And ensure they'd never find out who was behind all this.

The front desk was staffed by a woman. Dressed in a uniform of black pants and an emblemed yellow golf shirt. A smile crept across the woman's weathered face. Another minimum wage slave.

Kiki sidled up to the counter. "Hey, I need some help."

"What can I do for you, honey?"

"Well, it's my husband."

"Don't tell me. Mine left me three years ago."

"He's a deadbeat. Nothing makes him run faster than the sound of an alimony check. With his signature on it."

"They're the worst," said the clerk.

"I really need you to help me." She gave the woman a description of Ridley's features.

"Sounds about right. He came in here this morning. I told him we usually don't take check-ins until two. He went and paid for double time. But I think he left about an hour and a half ago."

"Really?" she said.

"Yeah, he just pulled out of here. I don't

know when he'll come back. You want me to get you into the room?"

"No. It'll be okay. What's the number?"

"215."

"Thanks. I'll just have to come back later."

"You don't want me to give him a call?" She picked up the phone. "Here—I'll give him a call. Right now. See if he hasn't come back." The woman keyed in the number and pressed the receiver to her ear. "Nope, no answer."

"Don't worry about it. But if you see him, don't tell him I came around, okay? For all I know he's bringing a girl back. You know the type."

"You want me to phone the police?"

"No, he's not that kind of deadbeat. We're still separated. It'll be a while before I see any money."

"You just get every penny out of him, darling. That's what you got to do."

Kiki left the lobby and headed to room 215.

"I've done an infrared scan," said Tin Man through her earbud. "There's no one in the room."

"Is Tatyana in place?"

From around the corner Tatyana appeared.

A quick turn of the skeleton key and they were in. It was an ordinary hotel room with cheap floral patterned bedspreads.

Tatyana pulled out her gun and went in first. "Doesn't look like anyone is here," she said. "I'll check the bath, just in case."

Tatyana walked in and the door slammed shut behind her.

"What's going on?" said Kiki.

Tatyana banged on the door. "I'm locked in here. Some sort of device shut me in. Try your skeleton key."

Kiki did. No dice. The door was metal. She couldn't punch through it. "It's locked on your side," she said.

"There must be a key somewhere in the room. Try to find it. You can pass it under the door."

Kiki searched everywhere but came up empty. Then, in the drawer of the night table. Next to the bed. She found a Gideon's bible and a cell phone. Immediately she picked up the mobile and flipped it open. It was covered with something. A gel or goo. She put it down—

—but it was stuck to her hand.

She turned it on. What the hell?

"What's going on?" said Tin Man.

"There's a cell phone. In a drawer. Now it's stuck to my hand."

"Whatever you do," he said, "do not turn it on."

"Um, well..."

"I'm on my way there."

She looked down at the phone. A message had popped up:

> YOUR HAND IS COVERED
> WITH A POLYMER RESIN.
> LIKE CRAZY GLUE. IT ALSO
> DOUBLES AS A PLASTIC
> EXPLOSIVE.

A timer started. Counting down from one hundred.

CHAPTER 13.5

Kiki was panicked. She flung the cell phone around aimlessly.

SLAP!

It hit the side of the nightstand. Maybe she could somehow get the skin off. Losing the palm of her hand was better than losing her arm.

Tin Man rushed over. He'd run all the way across the street from the RV. With his laptop. He opened it with one hand. Grabbed Kiki's hand with the other. "Get your palm over the computer."

"This thing—"

There was a bang from the bathroom door.

"What's going on?" yelled Tatyana.

"There's a bomb stuck to my hand. In a cell phone."

"You're better off in the bathroom," said Tin Man. "Find an escape route. Or take cover. The explosion could take out the whole room."

"This is ridiculous," said Tatyana

On the lap top screen a window popped up. Tin Man's decoding program. "What's going on?" he said. "This is insane. The inside of it—what's left is barely a mobile phone."

"What do you mean?"

The timer clicked down...47...46...45...

"There's no way to get this off. I don't know... what to do." He practically ripped his hair out. Opening another program, he took an x-ray of the telephone. "I don't know where to start—"

BANG!

Tatyana slammed open the bathroom door. "What is going on?"

18...17...16...

"The phone in Kiki's hand is about to explode. There's nothing we can do."

"Go," said Kiki. "Both of you. Get out of here. Tell my parents I still love them. Okay?"

Tatyana examined the cell phone. "This is a bomb?"

"Yes," said Tin Man, exasperated. "There's no way to get it off."

"Here." Tatyana grabbed Kiki's wrist and dragged her away from Tin Man. "Get out of here," she said to him.

"Where are you going?"

"Go. Now," she said.

9...7...6...

She dragged Kiki into the bathroom. To the tub. Threw her in. Plugged the drain. Ran the cold water.

4...3...2...

"Put the cell in the water," Tatyana commanded.

Kiki lay it down. There was a crackling sound. The screen reached 2 on the count-down and went black.

The two girls sat there in petrified silence. Nearly a minute elapsed. No explosion.

"Hey," yelled Tin Man, "what are you two doing in there? Taking a shower together?"

CHAPTER 13.6

"The thing about bomb makers," said Tatyana, "is the ones who design the cheapest and easiest to assemble are all in the Middle East. Not a place where they worry about excessive moisture."

They were on the road again an hour later. They had scoured—carefully—the room for other booby traps left behind. None were found, nor was any other evidence of Ridley's presence.

Tin Man drove while Tatyana sat in the back, trying to remove the phone from Kiki's hand. An acetone-dipped cotton swab seemed to be doing the trick. But it was slow going.

"Something about this doesn't feel right," said Kiki. "He'd never do something like this—"

"Really?"

"This isn't like Ridley."

Tatyana paused her blotting of the acetone. "Excuse me?"

"I just can't imagine that he'd want to kill me."

"How the hell do you know what he wants

or doesn't want?" Tatyana was clearly not impressed with Kiki's reasoning. "You dated him for six months. The whole time he was a traitor. His background was a complete fabrication. We still don't know where he came from. Yet somehow you're an expert on what constitutes his typical behavior?"

"Why would he kill me?"

"Maybe he doesn't love you. And maybe you have to face that."

"I don't believe it for a second."

"It makes perfect sense. He knows you're pursuing him and he laid a trap. Any one of us could have picked up that phone. Or a CIA agent. Anything to create a distraction. You've got to get this through your head. The guy didn't love you. Or he wouldn't have let you get in harm's way."

"But he wanted me on that helicopter."

"Yeah. And he might have tossed you out before they got to the airport. Do you think you could just go on your merry way if you had betrayed all of us?"

"No—"

"These people always turn on each other."

"Not always."

"Yeah they do. Because they're one step away from being shot in the back by their associates. They're corrupt. The only advantage you and I have is that we play by the rules. And we apply the rules the same way to everybody. The only reason I do this job is because my parents told me about the corruption in the old Soviet republic."

"I haven't even been paid yet."

"That's not the point."

"Then what is?"

Tatyana resumed dabbing the cotton swab. "Can I tell you a secret?"

"Sure."

"Promise you won't repeat this. To anyone. As in, I never said nothing."

"Promise."

"They, as in Digby and the committee, think you have real talent. But that's a double edged sword."

"How?"

"Do you really want to end up like your grandfather? Or the situation with your father? I know about your family."

"Who else knows?"

"Me, Digby. Maybe Tin Man. That's all. In our group."

"Can we change the subject?"

"Whatever you say."

"Where are we going?"

"Cape Canaveral. To meet Digby."

"Have you ever been to Orlando?" asked Tatyana.

"Yes. Why?"

"I've always wanted to go to Disney World."

CHAPTER 14.1

"This is the place?" said Kiki. "I can't believe it. I never expected it to be out in the country."

The RV was speeding along the NASA Causeway. A sliver of dry land between two great expanses of water. Hemmed in from the ocean by Cape Canaveral. The water gave way to forest and swamp as they approached mission control.

"It's like we're heading to the airport," said Tatyana.

"Have you ever been to a space launch in Russia?" asked Tin Man.

"I am not Russian. I am Estonian. And no, I haven't been to the hinterland of Kazakhstan. If that's what you're asking."

Tin Man smiled. "Better than the British. We consider ourselves lucky if we can operate a biplane."

The road seemed to go on forever. Passing miles of swamp and woods. "Well," said Kiki, "I guess that makes sense. No one wants to live next to a launch site."

"Apparently, said Tin Man, "fifty years ago there was nothing here. Then overnight, the whole space coast thing just popped out of nowhere. To think it's all going to be over soon."

"You think so?" said Kiki.

"They've stopped doing shuttle launches. Renting out space to aerospace companies. The government has no need for it."

"Aren't they going to do another mission in a few years?" she said

"They say that, but who knows? They're still doing satellite launches. You see—" Tin Man pointed far off to the left— "way over there is where they keep the rockets. They bring them in on trucks. And put them together in that big building. It's basically like an assembly shop for rockets. On a huge flatbed truck. Then they roll it out onto a launch pad. And then up it goes."

"Pretty cool."

"Right now they're constructing the largest rocket in human history. For the Aries mission." Tin Man leaned back. "It would be awesome to be a rocket scientist."

"Awesome?" said Tatyana. "Not very awesome. Sounds like hell to me. Sitting on a bomb. Waiting to go up in the air. Not my sort of thing."

"Yeah," said Kiki, "if you've see the hair on those girls who go up into space, it's not nice to look at."

They reached a gate. "Hey," said Tin Man to the guy, "this is going to sound really strange..." After explaining their story the man made a few calls. They were told to pull over to the side of the road. They waited at least an hour before the guard came over to the motor home. He handed them a parking pass and gave instructions where to go.

"They must really think the communists are trying to break in," said Tin Man once they were underway. "Three foreigners show up in a Winnebago. Not exactly welcoming, are they?"

They got to the front gate of the main mission control complex. They were directed to a spot between two tour buses. "Well that's great," said Kiki, "we're right here with the elementary schools."

Digby met them at the entrance. "You guys just had to come down here, didn't you? I've been waiting days for an appointment, and your arrive in time to be my entourage."

"Consider yourself lucky," said Tatyana.

Digby's face turned serious. "I heard about the hotel."

"Yeah, well," said Kiki, "I guess he's kind of lost to us."

"I always thought the guy was a homicidal maniac," said Digby. "Anyone who tries to fake their own kidnapping."

"Ah, there you are." It was Lieutenant Auster. His eyes were locked on Tatyana. "It is very good to see you. Mr. Saunders has said so many wonderful things about you all. Thank you for coming to NASA. But I must tell you that it has been very hard to get you permission to come into our control room. It might be several hours before it is all cleared. It has to go through Washington, you see."

"Oh, that's okay," said Kiki

"Perhaps you'd like a tour of the facilities."

"No, that'll be okay," said Digby.

"I'd really like a cup of tea," said Tin Man.

"I'd love a tour," said Kiki. "Can we go over to the rocket building?"

"Sure," said Auster. "I'll get you a pass."

"Well, aren't you the eager beaver," said Digby.

"It's good to know our surroundings. Just in case. And I might never get this chance again. I've never been to Florida," she said.

"What?" said Tin Man. "Not even on vacation? When most people come to America they go straight to Orlando. They assume the rest of the country is the same."

"Really?" said Kiki. "I thought they all went to New York."

"No," said Tatyana. "Even in Estonia, Mickey Mouse is the main place most people have visited."

"Isn't that great," said Digby. "Orlando. That's what our country means to the rest of the world."

Auster returned. "This is a pass." He handed it to Kiki. "You must show it every time you go through one of the military gates. But first let me show your colleagues to our canteen. There they can get anything they need."

"They don't happen to have beer in this canteen, do they?" asked Digby.

"Of course. This is a military institution. At least part of it. As you know, much of what used to be the mission control has been taken over by the navy. For our long-range surveillance aircraft. So I would request that you do not leave the canteen without my accompaniment. We wouldn't want you to cause any alarm with the military police."

Digby smiled. "Oh, we don't want to alarm anyone."

The canteen turned out to be a bar. Decked out in wood and leather. With a nautical theme. "Wow," said Digby. "I feel like we've landed in a dockside tavern. Straight out of nineteen seventy-one. Pretty impressive."

Tatyana examined the decor. "Plaid upholstery meshed with leather."

"It's amazing," said Tin Man. "I'd love to live in a place like this. I wonder if they have a decent fish and chips."

"Florida is not know for its seafood," said Digby.

"Anyway," Auster continued, "please make yourselves comfortable here. Meanwhile, if you do not hear from me, I'm sure Vice-Admiral McGraw can see to your needs. He'll be dropping by shortly."

"Vice-Admiral McGraw?" said Kiki.

"Of course. He is my commanding officer. Now, if you'd like to take a brief tour..." He beckoned Kiki to join him. "But it might be more convenient to take it by car."

"Sure," she said. "Lead the way."

They headed to the parking lot. A white Crown Victoria was waiting.

"This is your company car, isn't it?"

"It is indeed," said Auster. "I'm still getting

used to the American idea of large vehicles. This car in particular has a very rough sense when it comes to the handling."

"Oh, I don't know. They're comfortable on the highway."

"I suppose. Now, perhaps we should start with the cryogenic lab. It is the closest facility nearby. I can show you some of our latest experiments. To put people into a hibernation state for long space voyages. It is the cutting edge of science."

"Sure. Why don't you—"

Kiki was distracted by a grey Mercedes. The driver turned his head to glance at her. It was a mistake. She saw his face.

The driver of the car was Ridley.

CHAPTER 14.2

"Follow that car."

"What?" said Auster.

"That guy—in the grey Mercedes. He's the man we're looking for. We've got to follow him."

Auster looked at her with incredulity. "I'm sorry, we're going on a tour—"

"Get the hell out then." He was sitting in

the front seat, but hadn't closed his door yet. She grabbed his ID badge. Then swerved around and kicked him out. He stumbled back, stopping his fall with his left arm.

"What are you doing?" he said.

"Sorry, you'll thank me for this later." She turned the key over in the ignition. Auster reached up and tried to rip her out of the car.

BAM!

Her elbow smashed against his stomach. He stumbled backwards, winded.

"Sorry, you're getting in my way." She slammed the door, put the car in gear, and took off. She fumbled the pass in her hand. I wonder if they'll notice that I don't look like an Austrian drill sergeant, she thought.

Kiki gunned it. The car shot forward. Sixty miles an hour... seventy.... seventy-five... things were starting to rattle. Eighty... still Ridley was outrunning her. She doubted the Crown Vic could outperform a Mercedes with a two-minute head start. The needle hit ninety. She heard the supercharger kick in. Maybe she wasn't out-horsepowered—this must be the police model.

This thing could go out of control, she thought. She wasn't an expert driver.

Up ahead Ridley was slowing for an Air Force security check. He passed through with no problems. She looked down at her pass. If she slowed down she risked being shot at. She rolled down the window and threw it out. There was no gate to pass through. She floored it, shooting past the baffled soldier in the booth.

The guard ran outside, gun in hand. Kiki was too far away for him to make an accurate shot. He rushed back inside and phoned the military police.

In the near-empty canteen, Digby was still chatting with Tatyana and Tin Man. "We could be here for hours. Best we settle in."

"You want us to get drunk?" said Tatyana.

"Well, if you're not a drinker, you'll never fit in with these guys."

"We're at work," she said.

"Nothing is going to happen. This is day two of my wait for the Vice-Admiral. I expect it to continue well through day three."

As if on cue, McGraw appeared. "You're Digby?"

"Yes?"

"The man from NATO, in Amsterdam?"

"That's right. I'm glad you could take some time from your busy—"

"One of your people just assaulted my lieutenant and stole a car. Then whipped through a checkpoint."

"What?" Digby looked at Tatyana. She was similarly surprised. "There has to be a reason for this."

"I don't care. You better get a handle on this before she gets shot by the MPs." He sniffed Digby's breath. "You've been drinking?"

"A little."

"Well, you guys are really top notch."

It was a long silent march as Digby followed McGraw into the control room. He was impressed with all the monitors. "You guys sure know how to keep the TV business afloat."

McGraw turned to a nearby technician. "What's the latest?"

"Last we checked she was heading towards the Vehicular Assembly Building. The garage is trying to find the code for the vehicle's kill switch."

"It's taking too much time, tech."

"She seems to be pursuing a grey Mercedes."

"Who's that?"

"We don't know, sir. Its ID checked out. Captain Ridley Stockenhousen of command seven one five, Andrews AFB."

McGraw was pissed. "Who approved his clearance?"

"You did, sir."

"Well," said Digby, "it looks like I'm not the only one asleep at the switch. You better tell those troops to hold their fire. We've been covering your ass on this for a week."

"What are you talking about?"

"I'm talking about the drone you lost."

"We never lost one."

"Yes, you did. And they never informed you?"

"Informed me of what?"

"Of the fact that three days ago the agent who just stole your car—"

"Look, I don't need to hear this right now. We've got to deal with this security breach. And then you can tell me your fish story about a drone."

"You better not damage a hair on my operative's head. Or we'll never find out where the Daedalus is."

McGraw turned around in anger. "How do you know about that?

"Maybe you'd better sit down," said Digby.

Out by the rocket bay, Kiki was slowly catching up to Ridley. His car was pulling up to the tallest building on the base. Her phone rang. She ignored it. Then—

CLINK-CLUNK!

The car's engine shut off. For a few

hundred feet she was rolling. Then the brakes locked. She must've been at least four hundred meters from Ridley's car.

Kiki was already outside when she heard the sound of the doors locking. In the distance she heard sirens. She looked at the launch complex and ran for it...

At the drone control center the stolen Crown Victoria's dash camera appeared on the largest screen in the room. Kiki was running away from the car.

McGraw shook his head. "There's your girl. Making a run for it. Like the rest of those criminal punks."

Digby remained silent.

"Do we have an ID on the Mercedes parked at the complex?"

Before the nearby technician could speak, Digby interrupted. "He used to work for me. Decided to go freelance with a nuclear weapon."

"Is your girl there armed?"

"No."

"Why? Are you people afraid of firearms?"

"She's a terrible shot."

Kiki was out of breath before she got past the launch bay doors. She doubled over. It took a moment to catch her breath. She glanced back. A line of military police cars approached.

She found a side door. Ridley had planned this perfectly. The complex was empty. He'd waited until a Sunday afternoon. With no tours scheduled. She passed through the entrance. Even in the darkness, she was shocked by what she saw.

In front of her was a gigantic half-built rocket. All around it, a mesh network of scaffolding. Illuminated by a faint blue light. It gave the room the feel of a giant beehive. Except instead of honey and wax it was made of metal.

Kiki looked around. The place was vast and deserted. And dark. While her eyes adjusted she tried to find the stairs to the top. Or a doorway to a control room. If Tin Man was right, Ridley would have to get to the roof. She looked up and saw a figure racing up a nearby set of stairs.

BANG! BANG!

Kiki dove for cover.

CHAPTER 14.3

Kiki looked up. Ridley had stopped shooting. For the moment. She edged around the wall to the corner where the stairs started. The building was little more than a glorified silo.

A huge empty space. Where engineers who had assembled Legos as a child graduated to liquid oxygen.

How come nobody's here? You think they'd be a little bit more careful. With how much these things cost. She approached the bottom of the stairs.

BANG-BANG-BANG—

The gunshots were deafening. She took cover under the stairs.

BANG—

Another bullet ricocheted off the floor, then the wall. She couldn't see anything above her. She waited. The clang of footsteps. A door slammed. Then nothing. She was about to start up the stairs. Then she saw the elevator.

In the control room Digby was looking around. For the moment he wasn't in control of anything, so he decided the relaxed approach was best. There was no point in telling the military police how to do their jobs. He looked over at McGraw, watching the MPs speed towards the Assembly Building. "This is quite the place you have here. Is this the same mission control they use for the space flights? It seems awfully dark."

"This is a different room. Dark is better. People are reminded we're doing serious work here. If it was all bright and nice they wouldn't take their jobs seriously," said McGraw. "Now tell me, who is this Ridley character? Is he dangerous?"

"Very."

"Sir," said a crewcut technician, "we've got a visual from the top of the Vehicle Assembly Building." An image appeared on the wall. A wide angle shot of the roof. The camera zoomed in on a lone figure running to a small metal hut. "That's our boy," said Digby. "The one that caused all the trouble."

"The question is, why is he on the top of the VAB?"

"Maybe," said Digby, "you could ask my two associates sitting in the bar right now."

"He's got into the beacon control room," said crewcut.

"Can we cut the power to that?" said McGraw

"Uh, sir, we can," said Crewcut. "But it's going to take a few minutes."

"He went to a lot of effort to come here," said Digby, "just to get to that beacon. He's not doing this on his own. Someone here is helping him."

"That's ridiculous," said McGraw. "This facility is a secret even to top members of the U.S. government."

"Huh?" said Digby. "You give daily tours of this place for fifty bucks."

"Plain sight is the best camouflage," said McGraw.

At the Assembly Building Kiki burst on to the roof.

Empty.

Not a soul around. The door to the beacon control room was wide open. She walked towards it. Checked for Ridley. No sign. She went inside.

It was a small dark chamber filled with blinking controls and a bank of monitors. Lying in front of the main console was the drone control device she'd seen at the mine. It was all lit up. She got her phone.

"Sorry," said Ridley, "it's too late. What's done is done."

She felt metal. Pressed against the back of her skull.

CHAPTER 14.4

"There has to be a way of dealing with this. Other than arresting one of my people," said Digby.

"Your agent there has broken through two security gates. There's no way this can go unpunished," said McGraw. "We've got a procedure for this."

"You've got a procedure and it stinks. He sent a signal to the drone—"

"Our scientists are figuring out what happened as we speak."

"You don't have time. That thing could be hours, maybe even minutes away from destroying a major city."

McGraw was distracted. Digby's admonishment snapped him back. "Fine. I'll let your man over there have access our system. But if so much as a hair is put out of place on that machine, you people are out on your ass."

"That's a very wise decision," said Digby as the two of them walked over to Tin Man. McGraw arranged for the guy with a crewcut, Watson, to assist him.

"And what did you say your name is?" he asked.

"You can call me Tin Man."

"I mean your real name—"

"I'm afraid that's classified far beyond your level. Shall we get down to work?"

"Sure," said Watson, "but we can't just let you into the system with unfettered access."

"Well, you're going to have to. You've seen what's been going on today."

"Sure, but—"

"We need to find the signal that came out of that beacon."

"Well, from the data, we know a transmission was made. But it's been encoded. And not by us. It could take days or weeks to figure it out, if ever."

"Let's look at what I downloaded from those hard drives in Northern Quebec. Are you familiar with the operating system for the Daedalus?"

"Of course. I designed it myself."

Tin Man wasn't convinced.

"Building on previous architecture," said Watson. "Can I take a look at your computer?"

"Go ahead." Tin Man slid the laptop over to him.

"On the main screen is the text editor?"

"Yes."

"What's this down in the corner?"

"Oh, I'm trying to undo a mask applied to a phone call. The guy in the corner box made a Skype call from Sweden. I want to see what his face looks like. I'll have it pretty soon, I think. It's a regenerating algorithm they used for compression. Hard to reconstruct, but not impossible. He didn't expect someone would get a hold of the full resolution call. But I've got enough data to rebuild a frame or two."

"Lucky for you it's a static shot. Like a photograph."

"Exactly. Can you do me a favor?"

"Sure," said Tin Man.

"Get me a coffee. I need a few minutes to look through this."

When Tin Man returned Watson was even more alarmed. "You've got quite the thing going on here," he said. "This matches something in our database. But it looks like it's been corrupted. They've learned it. And they've rewritten it to do certain things."

"Like drop an nuclear bomb?"

"Maybe." Watson beckoned Tin Man to come closer. He lowered his voice. "This is code we actually had in the planning stages."

"Is that legal?"

Watson swayed his head equivocally and shrugged. "The bottom line is that we haven't completed it. Right now it's only supposed to do little things."

"Like what?"

"They didn't want the Daedalus to be able to drop any bombs. You see, it can go up to space. Sub-orbital, in theory even orbital flight. That's why the navy moved into NASA. But they wanted to make sure we weren't breaking any treaties by exploding nuclear devices in outer space."

"But they wanted that option coded for?"

"We have elections every two years in this country. If you want to keep your funding, it's good to keep your options open."

"Lovely place."

"Yeah, well, anyway, we put a kill switch in the coding. A series of directives."

"But what if you're not in control of the device?"

Watson looked around nervously. "It has, basically, a morality coding. A series of directives hard-coded in the operating system kernel. They activate once the device switches on. It won't attack friendly targets. Even if it's been hijacked."

"Like a set of ethics. As in, I won't hurt my master, you know, Asimov-style."

"Yes."

"What's the catch?"

"The program hasn't been tested. I only finished writing it two weeks ago. And I still haven't finished all the details for receiving instructions from the ground."

"But if they finished the program—"

"I'd have to see what's been coded. All you've got here is some half-complete execution line."

"What you're saying," said Tin Man, "is that we have to get to that beacon."

"Good luck," said Watson, gesturing to the screen. "There's a man with a gun up there. And fifty cops chasing him down below."

On the screen above was Kiki and Ridley—gun pressed against her head.

CHAPTER 15.1

Although the pistol was pointed at her, Kiki turned around. She looked right into Ridley's eyes. She expected a predator, ready to pounce. Instead she saw the gaze of the defeated.

She attacked. Punching him in the groin. He swerved to the side. She impacted his hip bone. Her fist radiated pain.

He knocked her aside. The gun flew away. He aimed a kick at her shin, but she bounced back. Flailing into the console with the blinking lights.

Kiki lurched toward him. "What are you

going to do? There's no way out of this."

He dove at her legs, taking her down. Banged her head off the concrete floor. She was dazed as he pulled her up and slung her over his shoulder. Then he bent down and grabbed his pistol. Ridley trudged out with Kiki on his back.

The darkness gave way to light. Her head knocked against Ridley's side, her nose rubbing against the fabric of his fake Navy uniform. She turned her head. Saw the aluminum-covered rooftop. All white. Her stomach was upside down, and nausea was building. At first she had felt dizzy, but it was subsiding. Now she just felt stunned, as anyone who'd just knocked their head off a concrete floor might.

She waved her arms around. It was the best she could do to fight off Ridley. But the bigger fight was against unconsciousness. She couldn't combat both. Part of her was happy, even relaxed at feeling helpless. Getting carried away. It was strange to feel so complacent. Kiki knew she should be panicked. But something in her knew he wasn't going to kill her. Even though her rational mind was begging her to escape.

Ridley stopped and opened a door. Back into darkness. As Kiki's eyes adjusted, she realized she was back in the rocket building. But they were climbing up. They reached some sort of catwalk. Ridley climbed higher.

Out of the corner of her eye, Kiki saw something. Adrenaline flooded back through her body. She was above the giant Aires rocket. Panic crept into her mind. Was he going to toss her off?

CLINK-CLINK.

Ridley's boots echoed off the metal floor of the gangway.

Kiki pounded against his back. "What are you doing?"

"Stay still, or I'll throw you over the side." He stopped.

Kiki's head swung over the railing. It was hundreds of feet down into the body of the rocket, an area of darkness. She lie still, terrified of what might happen next.

Ridley crouched down. Laid Kiki on the floor of the gangway before standing up and producing a pistol from his uniform. "Now," he said, "you think I'm going to kill you."

She looked at him. Feeling woozy she dabbed at her lip. Her tongue tasted blood.

He pulled the gun away from her.

And put the gun against his own head.

"No!" she said.

He pulled the trigger.

CLICK.

The magazine was empty.

"You would love that, wouldn't you?" said Kiki. "Let me watch you die. See all your guts and bone and brains. Right close in front of me. Show me all the pain you feel. Shove it on to me. Wouldn't that just be great? For you."

He gazed into her eyes. Defiant. "You have no idea about my pain. What I've been involved with—"

"I know exactly what you've done."

"No. You don't. Six months. That's how long you've known me. This goes far deeper. If you'd only seen me four years ago. Maybe you'd understand."

"I don't see how killing millions of people will help."

Ridley looked disgusted. "Shut up. This is pointless. I know there's no getting out of this."

"There are ways of dealing with the situation. You could be a valuable source of—"

"No." He leaned over the railing. Below cops were milling around the entrance. The sound of boots stomping up the metal staircase. Military police.

"They're coming for you."

"Right," said Ridley. "Once they discover there's an elevator."

He walked away from her. Then turned around and walked back.

"It'll be okay," she said.

"No, it won't." He grabbed her around the neck and pulled her towards him. "Maybe I do want to see you dead."

"Let go of me." Kiki's teeth were clenched. "Why are you doing this?"

"I thought I was doing something to make amends. And then I found out when you head down the road of death, your life doesn't last that long."

"That's not true. You might have valuable information."

"Yes I do, you're right about that."

"Maybe they'll do a deal."

"They might do that." He pulled her closer, again. "I'll miss you."

"Why are you talking—"

"I really did love you. Even if you didn't love me, I loved you." He held her tightly.

They fit together perfectly. She remembered the man she'd spent so many evenings with. Shy and awkward. No idea how dominating he could be. Part of her liked that. But this was too much. Not here. Not now.

"You know what?" he said. "I really wanted to hurt you. But now it's pointless, isn't it? You can't feel my pain. You'll just skim over it, like you always do. Superficially. Like every-thing."

Soldiers had reached the top of the catwalk. Ridley turned to them and shook his head. "You don't have to do that." He gestured for them to lower their guns.

"Get away from her," came the instructions from a bullhorn. "Surrender peacefully. We won't hurt you. We don't want to hurt anyone."

Kiki looked down. Ridley's hand was shaking. "So, what's it going to be, then?" said Kiki.

He pushed her to the ground and backed away. Then he climbed over the railing. Below him was the great cavern of the half-built rocket. "When they finish, it'll be the largest ever built," he said.

Kiki got to her feet. "Don't do this." She rushed toward him. "You'll regret it. You know you will."

"I'm going to regret the rest of my life no matter what." Ridley turned away from her and looked down. He let go of the railing.

And jumped into the rocket's abyss.

CHAPTER 15.2

It was the most sickening sound Kiki ever heard. Ridley impacting the bottom of the rocket. Like a pebble landing in an ice cream bucket. She looked over the railing, but there was only a circle of darkness below.

Then the screaming started.

"Ahhhh... the pain... the pain..."

Kiki looked down into the abyss. There was nothing she could do for him. She just felt numb. A little bit nauseous.

Something poked her in the arm. Next to her stood a military police officer. A corporal. His rifle aimed at her head. She put her hands up.

More screams.

The corporal looked down briefly.

Kiki heard more echoes of Ridley's agony. Like he'd turned his head. She looked to the soldier. "You've got to do something. To help him."

"He doesn't have long to live."

The tears came. Kiki tried to keep still, but she couldn't. It was like a geyser had welled up from her chest.

"Nyaaaaaaa..." This scream was quieter.

The corporal lowered his weapon. Gripped Kiki's arms, twisting them. Put cuffs on her. The metal cut into the skin on her wrists. "Come with me."

She'd managed to stop the tears. Now Kiki just felt numb. The corporal moved behind her and pushed her forward. Walking off the gangway.

There was more screaming. More desperate. As she got to the end of the catwalk, everything went silent.

Kiki couldn't handle this. She collapsed to the ground. Tears welling out of her. She sobbed, tears mixing with mascara. This didn't make any sense. She shouldn't be caring about him.

But she did.

"Kiki?"

Through watery eyes she saw Tin Man kneel down in front of her. And Watson, the technician. He beckoned to the corporal, who put his gun down. The two joined a third man, and had a conversation.

The corporal came back and took off the handcuffs. They gave Kiki a couple of minutes to recover, for her tears to dry. She buried her head in her arms for while. She looked up, and wiped the tears from her face. All she wanted to do was find a mirror. Kiki bet she probably looked like a clown right now.

Tin Man knelt down again. Passed her a tissue. "Are you okay?"

"I'm fine." She dabbed at her cheeks.

"No, you're not. But we need your help. This situation is really, really bad. This man with me designed the drone. He's going to help us. They're going to let you go. But I promised them you'd cooperate. Can you do that?"

She nodded.

"In a few minutes, a bomb could be landing on Boston or Montreal."

Kiki looked at him. "We've got to get back to the beacon. He wanted me out of there. That's where we'll find the answer."

CHAPTER 15.3

"This is it. This is the thing." Kiki, Tin Man and Watson were looking over the console. The very same one she'd seen at the Quebec mine.

"I can't believe this," said Watson. "It's a perfect replica. Except it's far smaller."

Kiki looked over the controls. Nothing about it was within her experience. "I don't think I'll be much help to you guys."

"Do you remember anything else from the mine?" asked Tin Man. "Were there any other consoles like this?"

"No," she said. "Just this unit. But it wasn't on when I saw it."

Tin Man took a closer look at the display. "The strange thing is the descent. How did they get it down? We have IDs on all the vehicles they used, and none of them had been at the mine site in the week before the drone landed there."

"What do you mean?" said Watson.

"How did they break the coding? How could they remotely land the craft?" said Tin Man.

Watson shook his head. "They couldn't have done that. There's only two ways it could take instructions. Either from our beacon here. Or if it was physically attached to another aircraft. While in flight."

"So it was hijacked from here," said Kiki.

"Impossible," said Watson. "There would be something on record. Some sort of evidence. I was there the night it disappeared."

"So, could they get a plane to hijack it mid-flight—"

"Impossible," said Watson. "The physics of that are near-impossible with current technology."

"But they did hijack it mid-flight," said Kiki. "Unless this was here the whole time."

"No way," said Watson. "The room is checked twice a day. This appeared when your friend arrived." Kiki looked away. "Sorry." Watson didn't know what to say, so he stuck to the facts. "He brought it with him. There's no other way."

"Then how did they hijack the drone?" asked Tin Man.

"They'd have to be physically attached to it," said Watson. "It's the only way the device will allow an incoming signal. Unless it's from this location beacon. If it's attached to a plane you could change parameters and mission objectives. But once it's in the air, the com system will know that."

"That doesn't answer my question," said Tin Man, getting frustrated. "How did they hijack it mid-flight? The only answer is that someone was sending a signal from the inside. From your control room."

"There is one other possibility," said Watson. "But it's classified."

"This is not the time," said Kiki.

"The air force has developed an advanced flying suit."

Kiki and Tin Man couldn't help but break into smirks.

"I'm serious," said Watson. "It's not very practical. They have a tendency to explode at inopportune times. The program was discontinued. But if someone got their hands on the prototype—"

"We're getting off track here," said Kiki. "We need to see if we can get control of the Daedalus."

"That won't happen here," said Watson. "I need to take this back to the control room and plug it in."

Something beeped. The middle of the three screens lit up with a map. "This is interesting," said Watson.

Tin Man shifted around to get a better look. "What is it?"

"It's just floating out there. Over the North Atlantic. At a very low altitude. Cruising along."

"Try to see if you can bring it back here," said Kiki.

"I'll try." Watson pressed some buttons. The whole unit went black.

Tin Man went bug eyed. "What did you do to it?"

Watson stabbed at the controls helplessly. "I don't know."

Kiki's phone rang. It was Digby. "Some people down here want to talk to you guys. We've started to receive some very disturbing telemetry. One of the Daedalus control stations started up on its own. The readouts say it's targeted New York City. And it's started a countdown. Twenty-five minutes before it reaches its target."

"It was all a trap," said Kiki. "This device—" she pointed at the console— "was set up to send the final command. It was waiting for us to interfere with it. When they investigate what went wrong, they'll look at us. As the ones who caused that drone to go off course."

"You mean," said Watson, "this was set up to make us look like we're the infiltrators."

"Yeah," said Kiki. "We've pushed the button that killed millions of people. While the real culprits cover their—"

"Stop it," said Tin Man. "You're both over thinking this. We have twenty-five minutes to prevent this from happening. Can we get this console to the control room?"

CHAPTER 15.4

The alarm rang again. "No, that's not it," said Tin Man.

It was Watson's turn to get angry. "There's only one way to hook this up to our system."

"What's the problem?" said Kiki. "There's barely five minutes left." They had dragged the remote console from the top of the Vehicle Assembly Building and rushed back to the drone control room. The clock was running out for New York.

"Here, one more time," said Tin Man. Watson flicked a switch. A line of code appeared on the panel's far left screen. Cascading lines of letters and numbers, just like Kiki had seen earlier in the beacon control tower. The stream of characters stopped, the screen flashed red. A command prompt raced through the words: Transmission Incomplete.

Tin Man shook his head. "There has to be a way to get the Daedalus to respond."

McGraw put down a red phone at a nearby station. He turned to them. "NORAD has just scrambled fighter jets. The drone's approaching the coast. It wasn't until they got a visual confirmation from a Lufthansa pilot that they agreed to believe us. This thing you invented isn't just a bomb, it's invisible." He turned to a technician at his right. "I think we can get a live feed. Can you put it on the big screen?"

Above them one quadrant of the giant display changed. It was the camera on the front of the fighter jet. It had made visual contact. The missile lock overlayed the image. They watched as the pilot locked on. The exhaust from the weapon appeared at the bottom of the screen, heading for the drone. The Daedalus easily avoided it.

"Like a missile chasing a missile," said Tatyana.

"It's coming back towards the pilot," said Kiki.

The screen turned to static. McGraw's phone rang. He took the message and hung up. "The pilot ejected." He turned to Watson. "Does this drone also use magic?"

Watson looked embarrassed. "It was designed to disrupt the guidance system of a short range weapon. We never expected to be fired on by our own side."

"Is there any way to take it down?" asked Digby.

"I'm not sure," said Watson. "It has all the latest technology."

"You designed this thing flawlessly," said Digby.

Watson shook his head. "This is what the navy wanted. It doesn't need to take orders from anybody. Unfortunately."

The timer continued to click down. The one-minute mark passed. A camera on top of the World Trade Center building came up.

"God, we're not going to watch it live, are we?" said Kiki. "All those people. They have no idea what's about to happen."

"I'd prefer to go that way. Not expecting it," said Digby.

Tin Man was still examining the console. "There might be something I can try. We can send an auto-destruct signal. I'm pretty sure I've figured out the command for it."

Watson backed off from his console. "Go ahead." Tin Man keyed in a line of code.

BOOM!

Everyone shielded their face. Sparks flew out of the remote Daedalus control console.

"It was the auto-destruct all right," said Tin Man. "Just not for the right device."

"Now there's no way to control it," said Tatyana.

"Doesn't matter," said Digby. "Time's up."

The clocked counted down. 5... 4... 3... 2... 1...

A small object entered the right side of the

World Trade Center camera. Kiki closed her eyes.

"What's it doing?" said Tin Man. "I thought it was supposed to... drop a nuclear bomb on the city. Or something."

Kiki opened her eyes. +15... 16... 17...

"It's supposed to," said Watson. "But it's flying past the city." He checked his display. "It just became visible to our radar tracking. It's gaining acceleration." He looked closer at one of his readouts. "And altitude."

In the left corner of the World Trade Center feed there was a small, but clear, burst of flames. "Look," said Tin Man.

"That wasn't an atomic explosion," said Digby.

"I'm patching this into the CENTCOM satellites," said Watson. A green display, like a bulls-eye, appeared on the wall. There were several dots at the top. A lone point was rising from the bottom.

Tin Man squinted for a better view. "It's using all its energy for a sub-orbital flight. How long before it runs out of fuel?"

"There's no way it could make it into orbit," said Watson. "Not after flying around for that long."

The dot reached the middle of the bulls-eye. Stopped. And began to fall.

"It's run out of fuel," said Digby. "It'll burn up."

The dot fell faster and faster, then disappeared.

Relief flooded the room. McGraw's phone rang again. When he hung up he was smiling. "New York is still there. They observed the drone breaking up."

The room erupted in applause.

"Great," said Tatyana. "All this effort, and it would have been better if we'd done nothing at all."

Digby was surprised beyond belief. McGraw had completely softened up. "You know," said Digby, "you can be a tough man. But I do admire you. After what we've been through—"

"If it's true what you say, I don't think it's my place to be judgmental."

Digby nodded. "We have to check out everything Ridley left behind in the beacon control room. Do you have a specialist you could spare?"

"Watson over there—" he indicated the technician talking with Tin Man— "has been our point man on the Daedalus project. I'm sure he can..."

McGraw was distracted. Digby turned around. The large video screen on the wall had changed. It was displaying a picture of what looked like McGraw. It took a few moments to register, but Digby realized he was looking at a freeze frame of the Skype conversation concerning Ridley's fate. "That looks an awful lot like you," he said.

CHAPTER 15.5

"Oh my god," said McGraw, "it can't be possible. It shouldn't."

"Can't be what?" asked Digby.

Kiki rushed over. "Get down—get away from him—"

"What?" said Digby.

BOOM!

McGraw's chest exploded.

BOOM BOOM!

More shots. Kiki grabbed Digby and dragged him to the floor.

Everyone was on the ground. Automatic rifle fire echoed off the walls. It lasted for about ten seconds. There was a metallic clinking sound as an empty magazine fell to the floor.

"Everybody stay down—" screamed Watson.

An alarm went off. Something flew through the air.

KA—BOOM!

The only doorway to the room exploded. Then smoke. And a pile of rubble.

Auster appeared through the haze, cradling an automatic rifle. He blocked the entrance. "None of you are going to get away. You're all in this together and you're going to die. Until we see the project through."

"Is that the Austrian officer?" said Kiki. "The one on exchange?"

"It is indeed," said Auster. He fired off a round of gunfire on automatic. In less than ten seconds the magazine fell to the floor empty. Auster replaced it in a single graceful motion. "To ensure that I'm taken seriously."

Digby reached into his pocket. Pulled out his gunmetal cigarette case.

"What are you doing?" said Kiki. "This is no time for a smoke."

"It's always time for a smoke." Digby got to his feet. "Look, what is your name, Lieutenant Oyster or something?" Auster aimed his weapon right at him. "I think we can do a deal. As a sign of good faith, I'm going to toss you over a cigarette and we're going to talk about this."

"There is no need to talk. You are all going to die. One by one."

Digby smiled. "Don't get so freaked out over things." He opened his case and picked out a stick of tobacco. "Just relax, will you?" He tossed the smoke towards Auster, who grabbed it.

"I hate American cigarettes," said Auster.

"That's too bad." Digby slammed his cigarette case shut.

PSSSFT!

The cigarette exploded in a cloud of tear gas.

Auster screamed, rubbing his eyes in agony.

"Everybody out," screamed Digby.

"No, you're not," said Auster, raising his weapon. He couldn't see, but fired anyway. Dozens of shots went wild. They all hit the ceiling. He tried to fire more, but the magazine was empty. Auster flailed around, searching for a full one. He fumbled for a knapsack at his side.

Of the twenty or thirty people in the room, almost all of them were gone. Except for Watson and the people from Task Force Ten. Tatyana and Tin Man were near the door.

"Go," said Digby. "You two get out of here."

"No," said Tatyana, "someone has to take him down."

"They have soldiers and police for that," said Digby.

"Those people are idiots," said Tatyana. "They'll spend hours negotiating with him. That's what he planned for. We've got to take him out now." She rushed forward and tackled the fumbling Auster. He resisted, so she kicked him in the shins. Tatyana grabbed his rifle with the freshly loaded magazine. Knocked him away with the butt of the gun. He stumbled back, while Tatyana dropped and rolled in the opposite direction. She turned to Digby. "Let's go."

She stood up and aimed the gun at Auster, who dove behind a nearby console. Tatyana laid down some fire, backing towards the door.

Tin Man and Digby got out. Then Auster re-appeared with a pistol.

BANG BANG BANG!

Tatyana dove out of the way. Kiki followed her as they scurried away from the door.

Auster took this as an opportunity to move between them and the exit. "I'll show you." He fired three more shots.

"Kiki," said Tatyana, "run towards the far side. I'll lay down some fire." She pulled the trigger. A stream of bullets sparked off a metal console. Auster fell to the ground.

Kiki looked at her. "What are you doing?"

"There should be reinforcements here any

minute. I want to get Auster between them and us."

Like clockwork a group of Military Police arrived. Auster greeted them with a grenade.

KABOOM!

The MPs scattered. Blood was everywhere.

He produced another grenade. This time he tossed it in Kiki and Tatyana's direction.

KA-BOOM!

Something happened. The room went pitch black. After a couple of seconds red emergency lights switched on. It looked like they'd descended into hell.

Kiki saw the figure of Auster in the corner of the room.

"Listen," said Tatyana, "we've got to sneak out through that door."

"But if Auster—"

"We can't win this now. They can send in someone with night vision goggles or something. We'll make a run for it."

CLINK-CLINK

Something metallic landed near Kiki. It bounced off a nearby console. "Uh-oh," she said.

Tatyana saw it. "Let's go, it's a grenade." She ran off to take cover. But Kiki didn't. She had put up with enough. The events of the day had made her go temporarily insane.

Something deep inside of her was tired of being pushed around. Turning her back to Tatyana, she reached down and grabbed the grenade. Hurled it back the way it came.

KA-BOOM!

Screaming. From Auster. Then a muffled gurgling.

The lights came back on. A team of marines barged through the door.

"Don't shoot," said Tatyana, dropping the rifle. "The target is down."

After a few words with the head of the assault team, they looked around. There was a dead policeman in the doorway. The room was thick with smoke. It stunk. Most of the workstations were a mess of broken glass and smashed monitors.

Then there was Auster. He was surrounded by a group of marines. Kiki moved in to get a closer look. The grenade had landed near Auster, but not on him. His left side was a mangled pile of blood, guts, shrapnel and the remains of his uniform. His face was peppered with small back specks of metal, all weeping blood.

He saw Kiki. "My fault," he said. "I picked the grenade that does so much damage. But not enough to kill a man."

It took another hour to sort things out and

get the control room techs back. Digby looked at them. "Who's in charge of all this?"

Watson raised his hand. "I guess I am, sir. McGraw and Auster were the only non-civilians in this section."

"How come no one in here carries a gun?" asked Digby.

"This is a civilian operation. The navy just rents the space."

"Well, you sure know how to pick your friends. We'd better hope Mr. Auster here doesn't die too quickly."

CHAPTER 16.1

The psychiatrist said she was from Oklahoma. Blond and middle aged. The demeanor of an elementary school teacher. Reminded Kiki of one she'd had many years before. While the woman spoke with a clear, standard North American accent, Kiki felt the words were coming out just a slight bit slower than she could stand.

"I don't see the point of any of this," she said.

The woman waited a moment before answering. "I think a lot of people care for you. A lot has gone on. They want to make sure you have a chance to express your feelings."

"Cut the crap. They want to know if I've lost my mind. I just watched two people die in the last six weeks. Yesterday I grabbed a live grenade. They're asking, how far will she go? Will she make a mistake if we give her a new mission?"

"Well, let's be honest," said the psychiatrist. "I've looked at the reports. You don't exactly get along with everyone. At least, not all the time."

"I've been getting along with people my entire life. I'm an expert in that department. Smiling. Pretending. Going along with things. Acting like I'm there to help out and be chipper. People treat me with a pat on the head. And I'm treated very well by a lot of people. But nobody takes me seriously."

"And whose fault is that?"

"Theirs."

"Really?" The woman scribbled a note down. "Why do you say that?"

Kiki raised her arms. "Look at how short I am. Not even five foot three. And small bodied. Every other person I work with is approaching five ten. And that's just the girls."

"That sounds like an excuse to feel inadequate."

"Really? This is your diagnosis?"

"You're using this insecurity as an excuse when your ideas aren't accepted by the group. By going out on your own, you're transferring your anger from their perceived mistreatment of you. It's your way of focusing it onto something productive."

"Maybe. What else do you want to know?"

"I don't want to know anything." There was an awkward pause. "How did you feel when your grandfather died?"

"I don't want to talk about it."

"Okay, well, that's it, then." The woman got up from her chair. "It's been very nice talking to—"

"Hey, where are you going?"

"If you don't want to talk about anything, there's no need for me."

"Sit down. I know how this works."

The psychiatrist complied.

"I have to confess my feelings to you. Then you put it into a report. Fine. I saw his truck blown up. Right in front of me. Felt the heat of the explosion. Within hours I find out I'm a prized commodity. Mostly because of my ties to my grandfather. I've inherited all his old case files. And his castle in Scotland. So everything in my life gets turned upside down. The only good thing that comes of this is that I'm not struggling for a job. I suppose that's good. I don't have to work that hard. That's a nice perk. I get to travel. Also good. People try to kill me. Not so good."

"Do you feel insecure about that?"

"To tell you the truth, I met a man. An ugly man. Who was older and unappealing. And sleazy. Tried to hit on me. On a ferry ride a few days ago. And I knew he was going to kill me. If I hadn't thrown him over the side. He's probably dead now. And you know what? I should feel bad about that. But the truth is, it felt really good. He was a bad person. But at the same time, I didn't enjoy doing it. Or maybe I did. I don't know how I felt about it."

"You're very certain of yourself."

"Oh, yes. He was going to kill me. Or rape me. Or seriously injure me. There was no doubt he was a bad guy. It felt okay to see him gone. Out of the picture."

The psychiatrist looked at her. Not knowing what to say next. She looked down at her file folder. "What if you killed one of the other members of Task Force Ten?"

Kiki leaned forward. "Look, I'm not a psychotic. I have emotions. I feel bad about things. I feel terrible about what happened to Jenny. I feel bad that I disobeyed orders and got her into trouble. And she'll be paying for that. Maybe not a lot, but a little. I realize I can make mistakes. That cause pain to other people. I get that the stakes are high."

"What about your ex-boyfriend?"

"I don't know," said Kiki. "He was lost to me."

"What do you mean?"

"There's only so much you can do for people. You can only take them so far. And then you've got to let them do the things their going to do. It sounds like a cliché, but I really have been to hell and back with him. There was a time, when I first found out that he was a traitor. I thought I didn't love him. I didn't feel for him. But there was something in me that didn't want to see him die. There wasn't anything I could do about it. He picked his own path. Turned against me. And everyone else. I stood up for him. I got him involved. To make his life better. And he used that against me."

The psychiatrist turned a page in her file. "Your parents live in—"

"Ah, no." Kiki stood up. "You do whatever you want. But I'm not discussing that. That was before I was employed by this organization."

"Okay. Have it your way." She closed the file. Kiki sat down. "You're going back to Scotland at some point?"

"Yes. I have to take care of my grandfather's affairs. I haven't had time to do that. I've been busy in Amsterdam and Barcelona and... it's been good to have something to do... and..."

Kiki broke into tears.

The psychiatrist walked over and gave her a hug. Let her cry on her shoulder for a few minutes. When it was all over, Kiki thanked her.

"At least I know you're a human being," said the woman.

Kiki dabbed at her eyes with a tissue. "I want to get back to work."

CHAPTER 16.2

Digby stomped down the hall. The corridors of the Florida Hospital were a perfectly white shade of paint, matched by the clinical hue of the fluorescent lights. He was in Orlando. It had taken him over an hour and a half to get here from Cape Canaveral. Through the muggy Florida climate and the traffic on Interstate 4. He was in a bad mood because he had to pay for parking out of his own pocket. And he couldn't get a receipt, either.

He flashed an ID badge at the nurse sitting

at reception. She directed him to the room. After zigzagging through several long, non-sensical hallways, he found it. Inside was Lieutenant Auster.

It was impossible to miss, with two police standing guard.

"I'm sorry sir," said the officer who had a head like a block of concrete, "we can't let you in there."

"Yeah," said his partner, an obese man bordering on middle age, "no one is allowed."

"You don't understand," said Digby, handing over his ID, "I'm with NATO. I was there for the fireworks show presented by the clown in that room."

Silence from the officers. The blockhead handed back his identification.

"I'm going in there."

"No, sir," said blockhead, "there's no way."

"Call your supervisor. Right now."

"Sir—"

"There's no way you can deny me access."

"We're only representatives of the Orlando police. You'll have to discuss this with the Navy."

"I don't give a rat's ass. You're going to let me in there. Right now. Or I'll have both of you fired."

Blockhead smiled at his fat colleague, who

spoke up. "We can't let you in there. We have a chain of command—"

"I can get both of you fired."

"Well, please go ahead and do that. But you're not getting through that door."

"I sure as hell am. I spent two hours in traffic to get here. You have no idea what I've been through. I've had guns put to my head. I've dealt with five different levels of bureaucrat. So don't give me attitude."

"Sir, you're not going in—"

Digby tried to rush the door. The guards grabbed him. He tried to resist. The officers hurled him back. He landed on the floor, restrained by both policemen.

"How dare you try to stop me—"

"Sir, if you don't calm down, we will be forced to place you under arrest."

"Don't you dare. I showed my ID badge. I've been through a lot."

Two nurses with a cart pulled up to the door. The fat guard waved them in. "Don't worry, it's unlocked," he said.

"This is unbelievable," said Digby. "This behavior. You want calm? Well I'm calm." The officers relaxed their grip. Digby stood up. "We'll see about both of your jobs." He turned around and stomped off. The blockhead rolled his eyes.

Inside the room, though, the nurses turned out to be Jenny and Mei. They walked towards Auster. He was intubated, barely conscious. Mei took out her stethoscope.

"So, what do you want to do?" said Jenny. "You're the doc."

Mei looked over his charts. "There isn't much they can do for him. He's going to die. No one could survive this."

Jenny saw Auster's eyes move towards them. "Are you sure about that?"

"His guts are being held in by Saran Wrap."

Auster gestured at a feeding tube, blocking his mouth. Mei removed it.

"So, you've come," he said, his voice barely above a whisper.

"You know who we are?" asked Jenny.

"Of course. You must be the ones who killed Giancarlo. And The Zebra."

"Damn right I am." Jenny grabbed at his throat.

Mei pulled her away. "No sudden moves. If his heart rate goes too high an alarm will sound. We'll have half the hospital here in thirty seconds."

"I'd like to string him up."

Mei glared at her. "Don't." Mei turned around to a tray on the trolley they had wheeled in. She prepared a needle with a clear liquid. Then walked around the bed to Auster's IV hookup and injected it.

"What is that?" asked Auster.

"It's one of our homemade medicines," said Mei. "Not commercially available."

Auster came to life. His heart rate increased. He smiled. "It's great."

"It's a narcotic," said Mei. "Enjoy it while it lasts."

"We want to have a conversation with you," said Jenny. "And we wanted to make sure you were awake for it. We want to know who's behind all this."

Auster chuckled.

"I wouldn't do that," said Mei. "Unless you want you intestines to spill out all over the bedspread."

Jenny moved in closer. "We have reasons to believe you have ties to South America."

"I'll tell you nothing," said Auster, "unless you do me a favor."

"What?" said Jenny.

"I want you to kill me."

"They might be able to save your life," said Mei.

"For what?" said Auster. "They've already taken off my arm. No dignified life is ahead of me. Others will come. Keep me from talking.

They'll kill me if I survive long enough for a trial. Or if they don't, I'll spend the rest of my life in jail. No, thank you. I have done what I wanted to do. I've struck fear into people's hearts."

Jenny stared him down. "Who is in South America?"

"You mean in Lima?" he said. "You have no idea, do you?"

"Don't play games," said Jenny.

"There's an army," said Auster. "An army of people lined up, ready for battle. He glanced around the room. All this will be gone. And these people. All gone."

"You mean they have another nuclear weapon?" said Mei.

"A nuclear weapon?" said Auster. "You are so naive. We mean to cleanse the world of you inferior races. You're an infestation. And we will start with America. The country you're trying to take over. The world is changing. And you're going to find out what it's like to be hunted. This continent will be given back to the animals. The trees. And the people who belong to it. There will be peace and order. Not the chaos and ghettos America has wrought. It'll be the greatest thing ever for the environmental movement."

"You're some kind of Nazi, aren't you?" said Mei.

Auster smiled. "I want to die. Inject me with something. Kill me and I'll tell you everything you want to know. Give me a death serum."

Mei went back to the cart. Filled up the needle. Injected Auster. "You've got about five minutes before your heart stops."

He smiled. "You'll find what you're looking for. You'll find it if you're a good tourist. Go to Panama. To the canal. I love tourism. I love Rio de Janeiro. I love Peru. So many good things. If you're a tourist, you might be able to figure it all out. Maybe Caracas, too. He started to fall asleep. I'm glad..."

"Can you wake him up again?" asked Jenny.

"No," said Mei. "It'll kill him. Or raise his heartbeat and set off the alarm. He'll be mad enough when he wakes up in a couple of hours and finds out he's still alive."

Jenny looked at the sleeping Auster. "One of us will be going on a long vacation. Those were some nice spots he mentioned."

Mei looked at her. "You mean, you believed him?"

CHAPTER 16.3

They were on the tarmac at Patrick Air Force Base. Just south of Cape Canaveral. The Cadillac Escalade emptied out. Tin Man, Tatyana, Jenny, Mei and Kiki.

"Well," said Digby, "we're going to miss you."

Jenny smiled. "I get vacation. But since you both speak Spanish, you two get the tour of South America."

"They speak Portuguese in Rio, you know," said Kiki. "And it won't be much of a vacation."

Jenny smiled. "So where are you going?"

"That's classified," said Digby.

"But first they'll be headed to Venezuela," said Tatyana. "They even booked a private jet. The Boeing 337-BBJ."

"I've enjoyed a BBJ myself in the past," said Digby.

"How did you score this?" said Kiki.

Digby turned to the plane. "It was a favor from one of the Admirals in the navy. They were quite gracious. When they discovered we prevented an all out nuclear holocaust."

"It's just us?" asked Mei.

"You two, a flight attendant and a couple of pilots," said Tin Man. "All at your disposal for the next six weeks."

"And a well stocked bar," said Digby. "I would assume you'd take advantage of it."

"I'm allergic to alcohol." Mei blushed. "How long is the flight?"

"Three or four hours to Caracas," said Tin Man. "It'll be fun. A little adventure. Just make sure you report in before you depart for the next city."

"And remember girls, there may not be a countdown clock on this one," said Digby, "but I need to make sure you know what you're doing. Don't waste time. Find out who these people are. We'll be working in Europe, trying to trace the money."

Kiki gave Jenny a hug. "You'll be okay?"

Jenny nodded.

"Say hi to Hawthorne if you bump into him in Baltimore."

"I'll do that."

"Be careful," said Tatyana. "You're terrible with a machine gun. And grenades." Tatyana turned to Mei. "Do not let her around grenades," she instructed.

"I'll do my best," said Mei.

"Where's Lisl?" asked Kiki.

"She'll be watching your back in Amsterdam," said Tin Man.

"All right."

"Carry on," he said.

They boarded the plane. Kiki sunk down across from Mei. A plush leather seat with a gold plated ashtray. "Look at this," said Kiki. "We can smoke. If we wanted to. Not that I smoke."

Mei smiled. "Tatyana would love it."

The flight attendant came by. She was a slender young woman of Hispanic descent. "We'll be taxiing soon. Once we've reached cruising altitude I'll be starting beverage service. There's also a copy of the Wall Street Journal in the seat pocket facing the aisle."

"That's fine, thank you," said Mei.

The captain came back. Gave an update of the weather in Caracas. And the estimated flying time. Kiki was impressed. Talking to the passengers in person. This was a first for her. "Quite the service."

"You've never traveled this way before?" said Mei.

"What? You mean, you have?"

"Once. When I was in Taiwan. It was nice. No lines. No security checks. We can take all our equipment with us. No hassle at all."

"I can't believe this is life at Task Force Ten."

"Enjoy it while it lasts. This isn't typical. With the budget we have, we don't get to travel all that often. Besides, weren't you flying Polish Airlines out of Barcelona? Or at least you were supposed to. Until you decided to make a detour to Canada."

"Basically, yes."

Mei rolled her eyes. "What a snob you are. They book you on a discount airline and you go off and disappear."

"Hey, it saved the free world, didn't it?"

Once they were aloft the flight attendant asked them if they wanted meal service.

"No," said Mei. "It's quite all right. We'll be fine. For now."

When the flight attendant left, Kiki looked up from the Cosmopolitan she was reading. "So where are we going first?"

"I have a contact in the Altamira neighborhood of Caracas. It's likely that some of these people are running money. Through the government there. If it's true, my contact can find out."

"But Venezuela's dangerous—"

"Very much so," said Mei. "You have to be very careful. Caracas is now the most dangerous city in the world. Worse than Kabul. But you do remember your karate, don't you?"

"Of course."

"You can't just toss around grenades whenever you feel like it."

"What about our accents? I'm not a native Spanish speaker."

"Don't worry. Leave it to me. At least you're half-Japanese. You'll blend in pretty well."

"True. There's all kinds of Nisei and Sansei in South America."

A couple of hours later Kiki's stomach began to rumble. Mei concurred. They decided to order lunch.

The got up and moved to the dining area. It was a booth against one side of the cabin. Facing a large screen. Playing a live feed of CNN.

"This is great," said Kiki. "We have our own little dining table. Are there their any movies on this thing?"

The flight attendant smiled and handed her a remote menu.

Kiki perused it. "Oh, look they've got The Breakfast Club."

"What?"

"You've never seen it?"

"Is it some kind of cooking show?"

Kiki rolled her eyes. "You have a lot to learn about the English language."

The flight attendant came back and set the

silverware. Kiki pulled off her napkin ring. As she spread the cloth napkin out on her lap, a piece of paper flew out and landed in front of Mei.

"What's that?" said Kiki.

Mei picked it up. "I don't know." As she examined it her expression changed. To fear.

She put her finger to her lips—be quiet. Something was up. Something involving the crew.

Kiki took the note and read the handwritten scrawl:

> THIS PLANE WILL
> EXPLODE MID AIR
> BEFORE CARACAS
> ONE OF THE CREW
> HAS A PARACHUTE
> BE CAREFUL WHAT
> YOU HAVE FOR LUNCH
> A BOAT WAITS NEAR
> GRENADA

Kiki looked over at the flight attendant, who had seen none of this. Then back at Mei. "What do we do now?"

"We watch your breakfast movie." Mei leaned in to whisper in Kiki's ear. "And keep quiet while I figure out what to do."

DON'T MISS THE NEXT EXCITING ADVENTURE OF KIKI CLAYMORE!

CODE NAME: CORONADO

Turn the page for a preview of
Code Name: Coronado...

CHAPTER 1.1

The plane cruised along smoothly over the Caribbean Sea. Kiki turned to the window behind her. A perfectly clear day. Sun streaming in. She looked back to the table where her dinner was waiting for her. She uncrumpled the note. Just to confirm she wasn't going insane, she read it again:

THIS PLANE WILL DISAPPEAR MID AIR BEFORE CARACAS
ONE OF THE CREW HAS A PARACHUTE
BE CAREFUL OF YOUR LUNCH
A BOAT WAITS NEAR GRENADA

Mei had already seen it and was keeping an eye on the cabin attendant. She glanced around the interior of the Boeing 737-BBJ. Provided by the American government, no less.

Kiki followed her gaze. So large. So comfortable. So... all for them. The only two passengers on board a plane that could carry a hundred people. To think it was Kiki's first time on a private jet.

Who would the killer be? she wondered. There were only three possibilities. The captain, the co-pilot, and the cabin attendant. Even if they could parachute from the plane, it was a hell of a risk over the open ocean.

Kiki hit a button on her armrest. The dining area faced a large, wall mounted video display. The image changed to the plane's exterior. There were four different angles to choose from. All showed nothing but sea and sunshine. She cycled through the options until she reached a map. It showed their start point, Orlando, and final destination, Caracas. A solid red line for where they'd been. A broken line for the rest of the journey. They were almost there.

"Looks like we're getting close to Grenada," said Kiki. "After that, Trinidad and Tobago. Then Venezuela."

"Yeah," said Mei. She leaned over and whispered in Kiki's ear. "Take the wet-nap from your meal tray. Use it to smudge your eye makeup. In a few minutes. Accidently."

After waiting a while, Kiki coughed. She raised the wet napkin to her face. Brushed it lightly against her eye.

"Oh, look at you," said Mei. "Your mascara is all smudged."

"Really?" said Kiki, loud enough to carry in the cabin attendant's direction. "I guess I should go fix it."

"Let me give you a hand," said Mei.

Kiki wondered how ridiculous this must look, but she couldn't think of a better excuse to talk privately.

Mei grabbed her purse and the note. Followed Kiki to the washroom. A place that was surprisingly roomy. Mei grabbed her phone out of her purse. Started a song of terrible Taiwanese pop music and jacked up the volume as loud as it would go.

"Why are you—?" asked Kiki.

"You never know who's listening," she said. "The real question is how they're planning to immobilize us."

"Gas?" said Kiki. "I saw it in a movie once."

"That sounds far too complicated. Getting access to the ventilation system."

"Bomb?"

"Too risky. Not something you do if you want to survive."

"Gun?"

"You couldn't shoot a gun off in a plane this size. You'd probably take out the fuselage. De-pressurize the whole aircraft. Never use a gun at cruising altitude."

Kiki stared at her reflection in the mirror as she reapplied her mascara. "Then we're looking at the food."

"Poison. Yeah. That works."

"What do you want to do?"

"Here." Mei opened her purse and produced a baggie filled with tissues and cotton swabs. "I'll put my bag between us in the dining corner. Take some of the food and put it in here."

"That's your purse."

"Worse things could happen."

"What about the drinks?"

Mei produced a water bottle from her bag and emptied it into the sink. "Put a little in here. Then we'll go back to our seats. If it's chloral hydrate, it will take five to ten minutes to kick in. After that appear groggy. Can you handle this?"

"Okay."

They went back to their seats and pretended to eat. Sneaking bits of food and drink away from the table. Away from the eyes of the cabin attendant.

With her plate still three quarters full, Kiki announced she wasn't hungry. Mei followed her back to the reclining seats on the other side of the cabin.

Ten minutes of silence. Mei closed her eyes. Kiki too. More time passed. She heard the cabin attendant approach. She got so close the Kiki felt the woman's breath on her cheek.

Carefully the attendant fastened their safety belts and walked away. That was a nice touch, Kiki thought. I'm much more comfortable now. Maybe she really did work for an airline.

Kiki squinted. She faced Mei and the forward cabin. She saw the woman enter the cockpit.

BOOM! BOOM!

Both Kiki and Mei opened their eyes.

"That was gunfire," said Mei.

The cockpit door opened. Kiki leaned back and shut her eyes. Mei stayed alert. Waiting for a confrontation.

The cabin attendant rushed past, without a second glance. Right to the back of the plane.

CHAPTER 1.2

Kiki heard the clunk of a plastic divider latching into place. It kept the lounge in the front separate from the rows of seats in the back half of the Boeing. To keep the rich separate from steerage, if you like.

Kiki leaned forward and tapped Mei on the knee. "What should we do?"

Mei looked around. "Who's flying the plane?"

They got up and moved to the cockpit. It was locked. Mei searched for a way to open the door. She got out her universal skeleton key. Provided by Task Force Ten. Guaranteed to open ninety-nine per cent of the world's locks.

It took some struggle, but she got the door open.

Inside was a sea of red.

Blood was splattered all over the windows and the wall mounted control panels. Both crew members had been shot point blank in the side of the head.

"Oh my god," said Kiki, covering her mouth.

"Put it out of your mind," said Mei. "Right now we need to get this plane under control. We've trained for this five times."

"Yeah, but against people, not corpses."

Mei scanned the controls between the pilots. "Look." She pointed to a panel. "The autopilot is still engaged. The engines are working perfectly. So the cabin attendant doesn't know how to fly the plane."

"You're sure of that?"

"Yeah. Why would you kill the pilots and let the plane keep flying?"

"Do you smell something?"

"Yeah. Acrid. Burning."

Mei looked down. "She's doused acid on the radio controls. We can't call for—"

KA-BOOM!

The cockpit panels lit up. Alarms sounded.

They scrambled back to the lounge. The left engine was trailing smoke.

"This plane should still be able to fly with only one engine," said Mei.

Kiki looked at her. "Do you know how to fly it?"

"This particular model? No."

The plane banked steeply. "We've got to find the cabin attendant."

BOOM!

The right engine went.

Mei steadied herself on the side of the seat. "Let's head to the back."

The plane canted downward. They were thrown against the dining booth. The two of them struggled to balance themselves as they walked back.

Mei reached the divider to the lounge and ripped it aside. The back aisles of seats were empty. The plane leveled off a bit. They got to the end of the fuselage.

Mei turned to Kiki. "There's an emergency exit in the back. You don't think she—"

"I hope not."

They raced through the rear galley and made a right turn. Kiki looked out a window. They were getting ever closer to the ocean. The airplane was now a glider.

One more door. It opened to reveal the cabin attendant. Putting on a parachute.

The woman looked up. "What are you doing? How did you—"

BAM.

Mei responded with a fist to the face. The woman shot backwards to the emergency exit. She grabbed the release handle. Pulled it forward.

A rush of ice-cold air pushed back against Mei and Kiki. The plane tilted sideways, throwing them both across the cabin. The attendant held on, got the door all the way open. Kiki saw sky.

Mei lurched forward. Grabbed the woman by the leg. The plane was canted to the right. The wall was now the ground.

She climbed up the attendant's body. He hands reached the clamps holding the parachute on. They struggled. Mei landed her fist again on the woman's stomach. The cabin attendant flailed wildly, kneeing Mei at every chance. Mei had her hand on the clamp that held the parachute on. She reached around it and released it.

The plane lurched downward and sideways.

A rush of anger flooded through Kiki. Everything became clear. They had to get the parachute or they would die. She lurched up, bracing herself with the back wall. She grabbed the cabin attendant's hair. The attendant kicked back. Pain ripped through Kiki's leg. Her grip loosened.

The attendant reached forward to get a grip on the edge of the open emergency exit.

Kiki grabbed the woman's waist, trying to get the parachute off. Mei had her in a head lock.

With all the force her body could muster, the cabin attendant flung forward. All three women fell out the door. Plummeting to the sea below.

CHAPTER 1.3

They rushed through the sky.

WHAM!

The cabin attendant kneed into Mei, who broke free. Kiki saw terror on her face as she was kicked away.

The attendant again flung her elbow backwards. Kiki grabbed the woman's neck. She reached around and clutched at the top strap of webbing. It took all her strength to aim her fist. It bounced off the attendant's chest. Harmlessly. Kiki could barely see, the wind was blowing so hard.

Kiki took a breath of air and focused. Tuned out the roar of the wind in her ears.

She reached up and pounded the woman's face. The woman flailed her leg back, missing Kiki's thigh. The cabin attendant was terrified. Kiki used all her energy to keep the woman's hand away from the parachute release. She got the left arm strap off the woman. She looped her arm through it. Gripped it as tightly as possible.

The woman would not give up. Another kick. Kiki felt a blow to her stomach.

Pain.

Nausea.

Uncontrollable nausea.

She couldn't control the rush of her stomach contents out of her mouth. The wind blew it back onto the cabin attendant's face. The woman reached up, trying to get the vomit out of her eyes.

Kiki punched her in the throat.

The woman fell out of the parachute. They flew away from each other. The straps only fit Kiki loosely. It was designed for a much larger man. She closed her eyes. Completely disorientated. She tumbled around and around, trying to get her right arm into the remaining strap. She couldn't get the clamps together either.

She opened her eyes. Kiki was upside down. Falling backwards. Flinging herself around, she looked over the horizon.

Down below her was Mei. Falling.

Kiki turned her body around. She held her hands out. Like some sort of super hero. Then she brought them together like she was diving underwater.

Mei got closer and closer. There was no way this was going to work, she thought. But it did. Her body was speeding up as she fell to earth. She aimed for Mei. As close as possible.

An eternity passed. She fell right into Mei's torso. Wrapped her hands around her. Mei saw her and smiled. Grabbed on for dear life. She wrapped her legs around Kiki. Slid her arms into the parachute straps so they were doubled up.

Kiki had no idea how much longer they had before the chute had to be opened. They might hit the water so fast they'd be killed.

Both of them faced the same direction. Mei pulled the tie clamps together. It was a struggle, but she got them connected. Reaching over, she grabbed the release handle.

They were flung backwards. Mei's head slammed against Kiki's cheek. She'd have a bruise there for a while.

They floated down to the surface of the water.

SPLASH!

Kiki was submerged. Mei grappled with the clamp, but got it released after a few tries. They struggled out of the parachute. Kiki's eyes stung with the salt water. Everything around her was blue. She looked up and saw the gigantic canopy floating on the water. It blocked out the sun.

Mei swam up, beckoning for Kiki to follow her. The water was as warm as a bath. As she floated up something nudged her legs. It was the back pack that had contained the parachute. It was floating up with her. It had released itself from the wires connected to the canopy. She pulled it with her. The cabin attendant must have planned to land in the ocean. There might be something useful inside.

Kiki broke the surface. She gasped for breath. Mei was on her right. "The backpack, it disconnected from the parachute."

"It might have a barometric sensor," said Mei. "A safety feature. When it sensed it was underwater, it cut the ties to the chute. We're lucky we got hold of it. The parachute might have opened automatically when it fell to a certain height."

The backpack floated by. Kiki grabbed onto it. She felt around. Probing one of the compartments. Mei ripped open a large one at the bottom. She saw orange plastic. At first she thought it was the reserve chute, but there was a plastic nozzle. She applied pressure.

The orange plastic expanded like a balloon. After a couple a moments they had an upside down inflatable raft covering them. It was small, no more than six feet on the longest side.

"Help me get it over," said Mei.

They flipped it and climbed over the side. They relaxed for a moment.

Kiki lay back. "How will they ever find us out here?"

"Are you kidding?" said Mei. "That plane is probably still gliding. It could go two hundred kilometers without engine power. We better hope it doesn't crash some place where there's people." She looked out at the horizon. "This dinghy is orange. And the size of the canopy... I wouldn't be surprised if we were picked up by the coast guard within a couple of hours."

ABOUT THE AUTHOR

Shane O'Brien MacDonald was born in 1980 on Cape Breton Island in eastern Canada. He speaks English, Japanese, and Chinese, and has a degree in economics and film studies from Queen's University. Before becoming a novelist he worked as an editor, cinematographer, and assistant picture editor on dozens of films and television shows. He has also been a foreign language instructor at the Tokyo University of Agriculture.

Mr. MacDonald is the author of the Kiki Claymore series of books, which have been described as "post-Ian Fleming female-centric espionage comic books in novel form."